Mary Roberts Rinehart

The Amazing Interlude
(Spy Thriller)

OK Publishing 2021

Mary Roberts Rinehart
THE AMAZING INTERLUDE

(Spy Thriller)

Spy Mystery Novel

Published by
MUSAICUM
Books

- Advanced Digital Solutions & High-Quality book Formatting -

musaicumbooks@okpublishing.info

2021 OK Publishing

ISBN 978-80-272-7770-4

Contents

I

The stage on which we play our little dramas of life and love has for most of us but one setting. It is furnished out with approximately the same things. Characters come, move about and make their final exits through long-familiar doors. And the back drop remains approximately the same from beginning to end. Palace or hovel, forest or sea, it is the background for the moving figures of the play.

So Sara Lee Kennedy had a back drop that had every appearance of permanency. The great Scene Painter apparently intended that there should be no change of set for her. Sara Lee herself certainly expected none.

But now and then amazing things are done on this great stage of ours: lights go down; the back drop, which had given the illusion of solidity, reveals itself transparent. A sort of fairyland transformation takes place. Beyond the once solid wall strange figures move on —a new *mise en scène*, with the old blotted out in darkness. The lady, whom we left knitting by the fire, becomes a fairy-Sara Lee became a fairy, of a sort-and meets the prince. Adventure, too; and love, of course. And then the lights go out, and it is the same old back drop again, and the lady is back by the fire-but with a memory.

This is the story of Sara Lee Kennedy's memory-and of something more.

The early days of the great war saw Sara Lee playing her part in the setting of a city in Pennsylvania. An ugly city, but a wealthy one. It is only fair to Sara Lee to say that she shared in neither quality. She was far from ugly, and very, very far from rich. She had started her part with a full stage, to carry on the figure, but one by one they had gone away into the wings and had not come back. At nineteen she was alone knitting by the fire, with no idea whatever that the back drop was of painted net, and that beyond it, waiting for its moment, was the forest of adventure. A strange forest, too-one that Sara Lee would not have recognised as a forest. And a prince of course-but a prince as strange and mysterious as the forest.

The end of December, 1914, found Sara Lee quite contented. If it was resignation rather than content, no one but Sara Lee knew the difference. Knitting, too; but not for soldiers. She was, to be candid, knitting an afghan against an interesting event which involved a friend of hers.

Sara Lee rather deplored the event-in her own mind, of course, for in her small circle young unmarried women accepted the major events of life without question, and certainly without conversation. She never, for instance, allowed her Uncle James, with whom she lived, to see her working at the afghan; and even her Aunt Harriet had supposed it to be a sweater until it assumed uncompromising proportions.

Sara Lee's days, up to the twentieth of December, 1914, had been much alike. In the mornings she straightened up her room, which she had copied from one in a woman's magazine, with the result that it gave somehow the impression of a baby's bassinet, being largely dotted Swiss and ribbon. Yet in a way it was a perfect setting for Sara Lee herself. It was fresh and virginal, and very, very neat and white. A resigned little room, like Sara Lee, resigned to being tucked away in a corner and to having no particular outlook. Peaceful, too.

Sometimes in the morning between straightening her room and going to the market for Aunt Harriet, Sara Lee looked at a newspaper. So she knew there was a war. She read the headings, and when the matter came up for mention at the little afternoon bridge club, as it did now and then after the prizes were distributed, she always said "Isn't it horrible!" and changed the subject.

On the night of the nineteenth of December Sara Lee had read her chapter in the Bible-she read it through once each year-and had braided down her hair, which was as smooth and shining and lovely as Sara Lee herself, and had raised her window for the night when Aunt Harriet came in. Sara Lee did not know, at first, that she had a visitor. She stood looking out toward the east, until Aunt Harriet touched her on the arm.

"What in the world!" said Aunt Harriet. "A body would suppose it was August."

"I was just thinking," said Sara Lee.

"You'd better do your thinking in bed. Jump in and I'll put out your light."

So Sara Lee got into her white bed with the dotted Swiss valance, and drew the covers to her chin, and looked a scant sixteen. Aunt Harriet, who was an unsentimental woman, childless and diffident, found her suddenly very appealing there in her smooth bed, and did an unexpected thing. She kissed her. Then feeling extremely uncomfortable she put out the light and went to the door. There she paused.

"Thinking!" she said. "What about, Sara Lee?"

Perhaps it was because the light was out that Sara Lee became articulate. Perhaps it was because things that had been forming in her young mind for weeks had at last crystallized into words. Perhaps it was because of a picture she had happened on that day, of a boy lying wounded somewhere on a battlefield and calling "Mother!"

"About-over there," she said rather hesitatingly. "And about Anna."

"Over there?"

"The war," said Sara Lee. "I was just thinking about all those women over there-like Anna, you know. They-they had babies, and got everything ready for them. And then the babies grew up, and they're all getting killed."

"It's horrible," said Aunt Harriet. "Do you want another blanket? It's cold to-night."

Sara Lee did not wish another blanket.

"I'm a little worried about your Uncle James," said Aunt Harriet, at the door. "He's got indigestion. I think I'll make him a mustard plaster."

She prepared to go out then, but Sara Lee spoke from her white bed.

"Aunt Harriet," she said, "I don't think I'll ever get married."

"I said that too, once," said Aunt Harriet complacently. "What's got into your head now?"

"I don't know," Sara Lee replied vaguely. "I just-What's the use?"

Aunt Harriet was conscious of a hazy impression of indelicacy. Coming from Sara Lee it was startling and revolutionary. In Aunt Harriet's world young women did not question their duty, which was to marry, preferably some one in the neighborhood, and bear children, who would be wheeled about that same neighborhood in perambulators and who would ultimately grow up and look after themselves.

"The use?" she asked tartly.

"Of having babies, and getting to care about them, and then-There will always be wars, won't there?"

"You turn over and go to sleep," counseled Aunt Harriet. "And stop looking twenty years or more ahead." She hesitated. "You haven't quarreled with Harvey, have you?"

Sara Lee turned over obediently.

"No. It's not that," she said. And the door closed.

Perhaps, had she ever had time during the crowded months that followed, Sara Lee would have dated certain things from that cold frosty night in December when she began to question things. For after all that was what it came to. She did not revolt. She questioned.

She lay in her white bed and looked at things for the first time. The sky had seemed low that night. Things were nearer. The horizon was close. And beyond that peaceful horizon, to the east, something was going on that could not be ignored. Men were dying. Killing and dying. Men who had been waited for as Anna watched for her child.

Downstairs she could hear Aunt Harriet moving about. The street was quiet, until a crowd of young people-she knew them by their voices-went by, laughing.

"It's horrible," said Sara Lee to herself. There was a change in her, but she was still inarticulate. Somewhere in her mind, but not formulated, was the feeling that she was too comfortable. Her peace was a cheap peace, bought at no price. Her last waking determination was to finish the afghan quickly and to knit for the men at the war.

Uncle James was ill the next morning. Sara Lee went for the doctor, but Anna's hour had come and he was with her. Late in the afternoon he came, however looking a bit gray round the mouth with fatigue, but triumphant. He had on these occasions always a sense of victory; even, in a way, a feeling of being part of a great purpose. He talked at such times of the race, as one may who is doing his best by it.

"Well," he said when Sara Lee opened the door, "it's a boy. Eight pounds. Going to be red-headed, too." He chuckled.

"A boy!" said Sara Lee. "I —don't you bring any girl babies any more?"

The doctor put down his hat and glanced at her.

"Wanted a girl, to be named for you?"

"No. It's not that. It's only —" She checked herself. He wouldn't understand. The race required girl babies. "I've put a blue bow on my afghan. Pink is for boys," she said, and led the way upstairs.

Very simple and orderly was the small house, as simple and orderly as Sara Lee's days in it. Time was to come when Sara Lee, having left it, ached for it with every fiber of her body and her soul-for its bright curtains and fresh paint, its regularity, its shining brasses and growing plants, its very kitchen pans and green-and-white oilcloth. She was to ache, too, for her friends-their small engrossing cares, their kindly interest, their familiar faces.

Time was to come, too, when she came back, not to the little house, it is true, but to her friends, to Anna and the others. But they had not grown and Sara Lee had. And that is the story.

Uncle James died the next day. One moment he was there, an uneasy figure, under the tulip quilt, and the next he had gone away entirely, leaving a terrible quiet behind him. He had been the center of the little house, a big and cheery and not over-orderly center. Followed his going not only quiet, but a wretched tidiness. There was nothing for Sara Lee to do but to think.

And, in the way of mourning women, things that Uncle James had said which had passed unheeded came back to her. One of them was when he had proposed to adopt a Belgian child, and Aunt Harriet had offered horrified protest.

"All right," he had said. "Of course, if you feel that way about it —! But I feel kind of mean, sometimes, sitting here doing nothing when there's such a lot to be done."

Then he had gone for a walk and had come back cheerful enough but rather quiet.

There was that other time, too, when the German Army was hurling itself, wave after wave, across the Yser-only of course Sara Lee knew nothing of the Yser then-and when it seemed as though the attenuated Allied line must surely crack and give. He had said then that if he were only twenty years younger he would go across and help.

"And what about me?" Aunt Harriet had asked. "But I suppose I wouldn't matter."

"You could go to Jennie's, couldn't you?"

There had followed one of those absurd wrangles as to whether or not Aunt Harriet would go to Jennie's in the rather remote contingency of Uncle James' becoming twenty years younger and going away.

And now Uncle James had taken on the wings of the morning and was indeed gone away. And again it became a question of Jennie's. Aunt Harriet, rather dazed at first, took to arguing it pro and con.

"Of course she has room for me," she would say in her thin voice. "There's that little room that was Edgar's. There's nobody in it now. But there's only room for a single bed, Sara Lee."

Sara Lee was knitting socks now, all a trifle tight as to heel. "I know," she would say. "I'll get along. Don't you worry about me."

Always these talks ended on a note of exasperation for Aunt Harriet. For Sara Lee's statement that she could manage would draw forth a plaintive burst from the older woman.

"If only you'd marry Harvey," she would say. "I don't know what's come over you. You used to like him well enough."

"I still like him."

"I've seen you jump when the telephone bell rang. Your Uncle James often spoke about it. He noticed more than most people thought." She followed Sara Lee's eyes down the street to where Anna was wheeling her baby slowly up and down. Even from that distance Sara Lee could see the bit of pink which was the bow on her afghan. "I believe you're afraid."

"Afraid?"

"Of having children," accused Aunt Harriet fretfully.

Sara Lee colored.

"Perhaps I am," she said; "but not the sort of thing you think. I just don't see the use of it, that's all. Aunt Harriet, how long does it take to become a hospital nurse?"

"Mabel Andrews was three years. It spoiled her looks too. She used to be a right pretty girl."

"Three years," Sara Lee reflected. "By that time —"

The house was very quiet and still those days. There was an interlude of emptiness and order, of long days during which Aunt Harriet alternately grieved and planned, and Sara Lee thought of many things. At the Red Cross meetings all sorts of stories were circulated; the Belgian atrocity tales had just reached the country, and were spreading like wildfire. There were arguments and disagreements. A girl named Schmidt was militant against them and soon found herself a small island of defiance entirely surrounded by disapproval. Mabel Andrews came once to a meeting and in businesslike fashion explained the Red Cross dressings and gave a lesson in bandaging. Forerunner of the many first-aid classes to come was that hour of Mabel's, and made memorable by one thing she said.

"You might as well all get busy and learn to do such things," she stated in her brisk voice. "One of our *internes* is over there, and he says we'll be in it before spring."

After the meeting Sara Lee went up to Mabel and put a hand on her arm.

"Are you going?" she asked.

"Leaving day after to-morrow. Why?"

"I —couldn't I be useful over there?"

Mabel smiled rather grimly. "What can you do?"

"I can cook."

"Only men cooks, my dear. What else?"

"I could clean up, couldn't I? There must be something. I'd do anything I could. Don't they have people to wash dishes and-all that?"

Mabel was on doubtful ground there. She knew of a woman who had been permitted to take over her own automobile, paying all her expenses and buying her own tires and gasoline.

"She carries supplies to small hospitals in out-of-the-way places," she said. "But I don't suppose you can do that, Sara Lee, can you?"

However, she gave Sara Lee a New York address, and Sara Lee wrote and offered herself. She said nothing to Aunt Harriet, who had by that time elected to take Edgar's room at Cousin Jennie's and was putting Uncle James' clothes in tearful order to send to Belgium. After a time she received a reply.

"We have put your name on our list of volunteers," said the letter, "but of course you understand that only trained workers are needed now. France and England are full of untrained women who are eager to help."

It was that night that Sara Lee became engaged to Harvey.

Sara Lee's attitude toward Harvey was one that she never tried to analyze. When he was not with her she thought of him tenderly, romantically. This was perhaps due to the photograph of him on her mantel. There was a dash about the picture rather lacking in the original, for it was a profile, and in it the young man's longish hair, worn pompadour, the slight thrust forward of the head, the arch of the nostrils, —gave him a sort of tense eagerness, a look of running against the wind. From the photograph Harvey might have been a gladiator; as a matter of fact he was a bond salesman.

So during the daytime Sara Lee looked-at intervals-at the photograph, and got that feel of drive and force. And in the evenings Harvey came, and she lost it. For, outside of a frame, he became a rather sturdy figure, of no romance, but of a comforting solidity. A kindly young man, with a rather wide face and hands disfigured as to fingers by much early baseball. He had heavy shoulders, the sort a girl might rely on to carry many burdens. A younger and tidier Uncle James, indeed-the same cheery manner, the same robust integrity, and the same small ambition.

To earn enough to keep those dependent on him, and to do it fairly; to tell the truth and wear clean linen and not run into debt; and to marry Sara Lee and love and cherish her all his life-this was Harvey. A plain and likable man, a lover and husband to be sure of. But —

He came that night to see Sara Lee. There was nothing unusual about that. He came every night. But he came that night full of determination. That was not unusual, either, but it had not carried him far. He had no idea that his picture was romantic. He would have demanded it back had he so much as suspected it. He wore his hair in a pompadour because of the prosaic fact that he had a cow-lick. He was very humble about himself, and Sara Lee was to him as wonderful as his picture was to her.

Sara Lee was in the parlor, waiting for him. The one electric lamp was lighted, so that the phonograph in one corner became only a bit of reflected light. There was a gas fire going, and in front of it was a white fur rug. In Aunt Harriet's circle there were few orientals. The Encyclopaedia Britannica, not yet entirely paid for, stood against the wall, and a leather chair, hollowed by Uncle James' solid body, was by the fire. It was just such a tidy, rather vulgar and homelike room as no doubt Harvey would picture for his own home. He had of course never seen the white simplicity of Sara Lee's bedroom.

Sara Lee, in a black dress, admitted him. When he had taken off his ulster and his overshoes-he had been raised by women-and came in, she was standing by the fire.

"Raining," he said. "It's getting colder. May be snow before morning."

Then he stopped. Sometimes the wonder of Sara Lee got him in the throat. She had so much the look of being poised for flight. Even in her quietest moments there was that about her —a sort of repressed eagerness, a look of seeing things far away. Aunt Harriet said that there were times when she had a "flighty" look.

And that night it was that impression of elusiveness that stopped Harvey's amiable prattle about the weather and took him to her with his arms out.

"Sara Lee!" he said. "Don't look like that!"

"Like what?" said Sara Lee prosaically.

"I don't know," he muttered. "You-sometimes you look as though —" Then he put his arms round her. "I love you," he said. "I'll be good to you, Sara Lee, if you'll have me." He bent down and put his cheek against hers. "If you'll only marry me, dear."

A woman has a way of thinking most clearly and lucidly when the man has stopped thinking. With his arms about her Harvey could only feel. He was trembling. As for Sara Lee, instantly two pictures flashed through her mind, each distinct, each clear, almost photographic. One was of Anna, in her tiny house down the street, dragged with a nursing baby. The other was that one from a magazine of a boy dying on a battlefield and crying "Mother!"

Two sorts of maternity-one quiet, peaceful, not always beautiful, but the thing by which and to which she had been reared; the other vicarious, of all the world.

"Don't you love me-that way?" he said, his cheek still against hers.

"I don't know."

"You don't know!"

It was then that he straightened away from her and looked without seeing at the blur of light which was the phonograph. Sara Lee, glancing up, saw him then as he was in the photograph, face set and head thrust forward, and that clean-cut drive of jaw and backward flow of heavy hair that marked him all man, and virile man.

She slipped her hand into his.

"I do love you, Harvey," she said, and went into his arms with the complete surrender of a child.

He was outrageously happy. He sat on the arm of Uncle James' chair where she was almost swallowed up, and with his face against hers he made his simple plans. Now and then he kissed the little hollow under her ear, and because he knew nothing of the abandon of a woman in a great passion he missed nothing in her attitude. Into her silence and passivity he read the reflection of his own adoring love and thought it hers.

To be fair to Sara Lee, she imagined that her content in Harvey's devotion was something more, as much more as was necessary. For in Sara Lee's experience marriage was a thing compounded of affection, habit, small differences and a home. Of passion, that passion which later she was to meet and suffer from, the terrible love that hurts and agonizes, she had never even dreamed.

Great days were before Sara Lee. She sat by the fire and knitted, and behind the back drop on the great stage of the world was preparing, unsuspected, the *mise en scène*.

II

About the middle of January Mabel Andrews wrote to Sara Lee from France, where she was already installed in a hospital at Calais.

The evening before the letter came Harvey had brought round the engagement ring. He had made a little money in war stocks, and into the ring he had put every dollar of his profits-and a great love, and gentleness, and hopes which he did not formulate even to himself.

It was a solitaire diamond, conventionally set, and larger, far larger, than the modest little stone on which Harvey had been casting anxious glances for months.

"Do you like it, honey?" he asked anxiously.

Sara Lee looked at it on her finger.

"It is lovely! It-it's terrible!" said poor Sara Lee, and cried on his shoulder.

Harvey was not subtle. He had never even heard of Mabel Andrews, and he had a tendency to restrict his war reading to the quarter column in the morning paper entitled "Salient Points of the Day's War News."

What could he know, for instance, of wounded men who were hungry? Which is what Mabel wrote about.

"You said you could cook," she had written. "Well, we need cooks, and something to cook. Sometime they'll have it all fixed, no doubt, but just now it's awful, Sara Lee. The British have money and food, plenty of it. But here-yesterday I cut the clothes off a wounded Belgian boy. He had been forty-eight hours on a railway siding, without even soup or coffee."

It was early in the war then, and between Ypres and the sea stretched a long thin line of Belgian trenches. A frantic Belgian Government, thrust out of its own land, was facing the problem, with scant funds and with no *matériel* of any sort, for feeding that desolate little army. France had her own problems-her army, non-productive industrially, and the great and constantly growing British forces quartered there, paying for what they got, but requiring much. The world knows now of the starvation of German-occupied Belgium. What it does not know and may never know is of the struggle during those early days to feed the heroic Belgian Army in their wet and almost untenable trenches.

Hospital trains they could improvise out of what rolling stock remained to them. Money could be borrowed, and was. But food? Clothing? Ammunition? In his little villa on the seacoast the Belgian King knew that his soldiers were hungry, and paced the floor of his tiny living-room; and over in an American city whose skyline was as pointed with furnace turrets as Constantinople's is with mosques, over there Sara Lee heard that call of hunger, and-put on her engagement ring.

Later on that evening, with Harvey's wide cheerful face turned adoringly to her, Sara Lee formulated a question:

"Don't you sometimes feel as though you'd like to go to France and fight?"

"What for?"

"Well, they need men, don't they?"

"I guess they don't need me, honey. I'd be the dickens of a lot of use! Never fired a gun in my life."

"You could learn. It isn't hard."

Harvey sat upright and stared at her.

"Oh, if you want me to go —" he said, and waited.

Sara Lee twisted her ring on her finger.

"Nobody wants anybody to go," she said not very elegantly. "I'd just —I'd rather like to think you wanted to go."

That was almost too subtle for Harvey. Something about him was rather reminiscent of Uncle James on mornings when he was determined not to go to church.

"It's not our fight," he said. "And as far as that goes, I'm not so sure there isn't right on both sides. Or wrong. Most likely wrong. I'd look fine going over there to help the Allies, and then making up my mind it was the British who'd spilled the beans. Now let's talk about something interesting-for instance, how much we love each other."

It was always "we" with Harvey. In his simple creed if a girl accepted a man and let him kiss her and wore his ring it was a reciprocal love affair. It never occurred to him that sometimes as the evening dragged toward a close Sara Lee was just a bit weary of his arms, and that she sought, after he had gone, the haven of her little white room, and closed the door, and had to look rather a long time at his photograph before she was in a properly loving mood again.

But that night after his prolonged leave-taking Sara Lee went upstairs to her room and faced the situation.

She was going to marry Harvey. She was committed to that. And she loved him; not as he cared, perhaps, but he was a very definite part of her life. Once or twice when he had been detained by business she had missed him, had put in a lonely and most unhappy evening.

Sara Lee had known comparatively few men. In that small and simple circle of hers, with its tennis court in a vacant lot, its one or two inexpensive cars, its picnics and porch parties, there was none of the usual give and take of more sophisticated circles. Boys and girls paired off rather early, and remained paired by tacit agreement; there was comparatively little shifting. There were few free lances among the men, and none among the girls. When she was seventeen Harvey had made it known unmistakably that Sara Lee was his, and no trespassing. And for two years he had without intentional selfishness kept Sara Lee for himself.

That was how matters stood that January night when Sara Lee went upstairs after Harvey had gone and read Mabel's letter, with Harvey's photograph turned to the wall. Under her calm exterior a little flame of rebellion was burning in her. Harvey's perpetual "we," his attitude toward the war, and Mabel's letter, with what it opened before her, had set the match to something in Sara Lee she did not recognize —a strain of the adventurer, a throw-back to some wandering ancestor perhaps. But more than anything it had set fire to the something maternal that is in all good women.

Yet, had Aunt Harriet not come in just then, the flame might have died. And had it died a certain small page of the history of this war would never have been written.

Aunt Harriet came in hesitatingly. She wore a black wrapper, and her face, with her hair drawn back for the night, looked tight and old.

"Harvey gone?" she asked.

"Yes."

"I thought I'd better come in. There's something —I can tell you in the morning if you're tired."

"I'm not tired," said Sara Lee.

Aunt Harriet sat down miserably on a chair.

"I've had a letter from Jennie," she stated. "The girl's gone, and the children have whooping cough. She'd like me to come right away."

"To do the maid's work!" said Sara Lee indignantly. "You mustn't do it, that's all! She can get somebody."

But Aunt Harriet was firm. She was not a fair-weather friend, and since Jennie was good enough to offer her a home she felt she ought to go at once.

"You'll have to get married right away," she finished. "Goodness knows it's time enough! For two years Harvey has been barking like a watchdog in front of the house and keeping every other young man away."

Sara Lee smiled.

"He's only been lying on the doormat, Aunt Harriet," she observed. "I don't believe he knows how to bark."

"Oh, he's mild enough. He may change after marriage. Some do. But," she added hastily, "he'll be a good husband. He's that sort."

Suddenly something that had been taking shape in Sara Lee's small head, quite unknown to her, developed identity and speech.

"But I'm not going to marry him just yet," she said.

Aunt Harriet's eyes fell on the photograph with its face to the wall, and she started.

"You haven't quarreled with him, have you?"

"No, of course not! I have something else I want to do first. That's all. Aunt Harriet, I want to go to France."

Aunt Harriet began to tremble, and Sara Lee went over and put her young arms about her.

"Don't look like that," she said. "It's only for a little while. I've got to go. I just have to, that's all!"

"Go how?" demanded Aunt Harriet.

"I don't know. I'll find some way. I've had a letter from Mabel. Things are awful over there."

"And how will you help them?" Her face worked nervously. "Is it going to help for you to be shot? Or carried off by the Germans?" The atrocity stories were all that Aunt Harriet knew of the war, and all she could think of now. "You'll come back with your hands cut off."

Sara Lee straightened and looked out where between the white curtains the spire of the Methodist Church marked the east.

"I'm going," she said. And she stood there, already poised for flight.

There was no sleep in the little house that night. Sara Lee could hear the older woman moving about in her lonely bed, where the spring still sagged from Uncle James' heavy form, and at last she went in and crept in beside her. Toward morning Aunt Harriet slept, with the girl's arm across her; and then Sara Lee went back to her room and tried to plan.

She had a little money, and she had heard that living was cheap abroad. She could get across then, and perhaps keep herself. But she must do more than that, to justify her going. She must get money, and then decide how the money was to be spent. If she could only talk it over with Uncle James! Or, with Harvey. Harvey knew about business and money.

But she dared not go to Harvey. She was terribly frightened when she even thought of him. There was no hope of making him understand; and no chance of reasoning with him, because, to be frank, she had no reasons. She had only instinct-instinct and a great tenderness toward suffering. No, obviously Harvey must not know until everything was arranged.

That morning the Methodist Church packed a barrel for the Belgians. There was a real rite of placing in it Mrs. Augustus Gregory's old sealskin coat, now a light brown and badly worn, but for years the only one in the neighborhood. Various familiar articles appeared, to be thrust into darkness, only to emerge in surroundings never dreamed of in their better days- the little Howard boy's first trouser suit; the clothing of a baby that had never lived; big Joe Hemmingway's dress suit, the one he was married in and now too small for him. And here and there things that could ill be spared, brought in and offered with resolute cheerfulness.

Sara Lee brought some of Uncle James' things, and was at once set to work. The women there called Sara Lee capable, but it was to take other surroundings to bring out her real efficiency.

And it was when bending over a barrel, while round her went on that pitying talk of women about a great calamity, that Sara Lee got her great idea; and later on she made the only speech of her life.

That evening Harvey went home in a quiet glow of happiness. He had had a good day. And he had heard of a little house that would exactly suit Sara Lee and him. He did not notice his sister's silence when he spoke about it. He was absorbed, manlike, in his plans.

"The Leete house," he said in answer to her perfunctory question. "Will Leete has lost his mind and volunteered for the ambulance service in France. Mrs. Leete is going to her mother's."

"Maybe he feels it's his duty. He can drive a car, and they have no children."

"Duty nothing!" He seemed almost unduly irritated. "He's tired of the commission business, that's all. Y'ought to have heard the fellows in the office. Anyhow, they want to sub-let the house, and I'm going to take Sara Lee there to-night."

His sister looked at him, and there was in her face something of the expression of the women that day as they packed the barrel. But she said nothing until he was leaving the house that night. Then she put a hand on his arm. She was a weary little woman, older than Harvey, and tired with many children. She had been gathering up small overshoes in the hall and he had stopped to help her.

"You know, Harvey, Sara Lee's not —I always think she's different, somehow."

"Well, I guess yes! There's nobody like her."

"You can't bully her, you know."

Harvey stared at her with honestly perplexed eyes.

"Bully!" he said. "What on earth makes you say that?"

Then he laughed.

"Don't you worry, Belle," he said. "I know I'm a fierce and domineering person, but if there's any bullying I know who'll do it."

"She's not like the other girls you know," she reiterated rather helplessly.

"Sure she's not! But she's enough like them to need a house to live in. And if she isn't crazy about the Leete place I'll eat it."

He banged out cheerfully, whistling as he went down the street. He stopped whistling, however, at Sara Lee's door. The neighborhood preserved certain traditions as to a house of mourning. It lowered its voice in passing and made its calls of condolence in dark clothes and a general air of gloom. Pianos near by were played only with the windows closed, and even the milkman leaving his bottles walked on tiptoe and presented his monthly bill solemnly.

So Harvey stopped whistling, rang the bell apologetically, and-faced a new and vivid Sara Lee, flushed and with shining eyes, but woefully frightened.

She told him almost at once. He had only reached the dining room of the Leete house, which he was explaining had a white wainscoting when she interrupted him. The ladies of the Methodist Church were going to collect a certain amount each month to support a soup kitchen as near the Front as possible.

"Good work!" said Harvey heartily. "I suppose they do get hungry, poor devils. Now about the dining room —"

"Harvey dear," Sara Lee broke in, "I've not finished. I —I'm going over to run it."

"You are not!"

"But I am! It's all arranged. It's my plan. They've all wanted to do something besides giving clothes. They send barrels, and they never hear from them again, and it's hard to keep interested. But with me there, writing home and telling them, 'To-day we served soup to this man, and that man, perhaps wounded.' And-and that sort of thing-don't you see how interested every one will be? Mrs. Gregory has promised twenty-five dollars a month, and —"

"You're not going," said Harvey in a flat tone. "That's all. Don't talk to me about it."

Sara Lee flushed deeper and started again, but rather hopelessly. There was no converting a man who would not argue or reason, who based everything on flat refusal.

"But somebody must go," she said with a tightening of her voice. "Here's Mabel Andrews' letter. Read it and you will understand."

"I don't want to read it."

Nevertheless he took it and read it. He read slowly. He did nothing quickly except assert his masculine domination. He had all the faults of his virtues; he was as slow as he was sure, as unimaginative as he was faithful.

He read it and gave it back to her.

"I don't think you mean it," he said. "I give you credit for too much sense. Maybe some one is needed over there. I guess things are pretty bad. But why should you make it your affair? There are about a million women in this country that haven't got anything else to do. Let them go."

"Some of them will. But they're afraid, mostly."

"Afraid! My God, I should think they would be afraid! And you're asking me to let you go into danger, to put off our wedding while you wander about over there with a million men and no women and —"

"You're wrong, Harvey dear," said Sara Lee in a low voice. "I am not asking you at all. I am telling you that I am going."

Sara Lee's leaving made an enormous stir in her small community. Opinion was divided. She was right according to some; she was mad according to others. The women of the Methodist Church, finding a real field of activity, stood behind her solidly. Guaranties of funds came in in a steady flow, though the amounts were small; and, on the word going about that she was to start a soup kitchen for the wounded, housewives sent in directions for making their most cherished soups.

Sara Lee, going to a land where the meat was mostly horse and where vegetables were scarce and limited to potatoes, Brussels sprouts and cabbage, found herself the possessor of recipes for making such sick-room dainties as mushroom soup, cream of asparagus, clam broth with whipped cream, and from Mrs. Gregory, the wealthy woman of the church-green turtle and consomme.

She was very busy and rather sad. She was helping Aunt Harriet to close the house and getting her small wardrobe in order. And once a day she went to a school of languages and painfully learned from a fierce and kindly old Frenchman a list of French nouns and prefixes like this: *Le livre, le crayon, la plume, la fenêtre*, and so on. By the end of ten days she could say: *"La rose sent-elle bon?"*

Considering that Harvey came every night and ran the gamut of the emotions, from pleading and expostulation at eight o'clock to black fury at ten, when he banged out of the house, Sara Lee was amazingly calm. If she had moments of weakness, when the call from overseas was less insistent than the call for peace and protection-if the nightly drawn picture of the Leete house, with tile mantels and a white bathroom, sometimes obtruded itself as against her approaching homelessness, Sara Lee made no sign.

She had her photograph taken for her passport, and when Harvey refused one she sent it to him by mail, with the word "Please" in the corner. Harvey groaned over it, and got it out at night and scolded it wildly; and then slept with it under his pillows, when he slept at all.

Not Sara Lee, and certainly not Harvey, knew what was calling her. And even later, when waves of homesickness racked her with wild remorse, she knew that she had had to go and that she could not return until she had done the thing for which she had been sent, whatever that might be.

III

The first thing that struck Sara Lee was the way she was saying her nightly prayers in all sorts of odd places. In trains and in hotels and, after sufficient interval, in the steamer. She prayed under these novel circumstances to be made a better girl, and to do a lot of good over there, and to be forgiven for hurting Harvey. She did this every night, and then got into her narrow bed and studied French nouns-because she had decided that there was no time for verbs-and numbers, which put her to sleep.

"Un, deux, trois, quatre, cinq," Sara Lee would begin, and go on, rocking gently in her berth as the steamer rolled, "Vingt, vingt-et-un, vingt-deux, trente, trente-et-un —" Her voice would die away. The book on the floor and Harvey's picture on the tiny table, Sara Lee would sleep. And as the ship trembled the light over her head would shine on Harvey's ring, and it glistened like a tear.

One thing surprised her as she gradually met some of her fellow passengers. She was not alone on her errand. Others there were on board, young and old women, and men, too, who had felt the call of mercy and were going, as ignorant as she, to help. As ignorant, but not so friendless. Most of them were accredited somewhere. They had definite objectives. But what was more alarming-they talked in big figures. Great organizations were behind them. She heard of the rehabilitation of Belgium, and portable hospitals, and millions of dollars, and Red Cross trains.

Not once did Sara Lee hear of anything so humble as a soup kitchen. The war was a vast thing, they would observe. It could only be touched by great organizations. Individual effort was negligible.

Once she took her courage in her hands.

"But I should think," she said, "that even great organizations depend on the-on individual efforts."

The portable hospital woman turned to her patronizingly.

"Certainly, my dear," she said. "But coördinated-coördinated."

It is hard to say just when the lights went down on Sara Lee's quiet stage and the interlude began. Not on the steamer, for after three days of discouragement and good weather they struck a storm; and Sara Lee's fine frenzy died for a time, of nausea. She did not appear again until the boat entered the Mersey, a pale and shaken angel of mercy, not at all sure of her wings, and most terribly homesick.

That night Sara Lee made a friend, one that Harvey would have approved of, an elderly Englishman named Travers. He was standing by the rail in the rain looking out at the blinking signal lights on both sides of the river. The ship for the first time had abandoned its policy of darkness and the decks were bathed in light.

Overhead the yardarm blinkers were signaling, and directly over Sara Lee's head a great white searchlight swept the water ahead. The wind was blowing a gale, and the red and green lights of the pilot boat swung in great arcs that seemed to touch the waves on either side.

Sara Lee stood beside Mr. Travers, for companionship only. He had preserved a typically British aloofness during the voyage, and he had never spoken to her. But there was something forlorn in Sara Lee that night as she clutched her hat with both hands and stared out at the shore lights. And if he had been silent during the voyage he had not been deaf. So he knew why almost every woman on the ship was making the voyage; but he knew nothing about Sara Lee.

"Bad night," said Mr. Travers.

"I was wondering what they are trying to do with that little boat."

Mr. Travers concealed the surprise of a man who was making his seventy-second voyage.

"That's the pilot boat," he explained. "We are picking up a pilot."

"But," marveled Sara Lee rather breathlessly, "have we come all the way without any pilot?"

He explained that to her, and showed her a few moments later how the pilot came with incredible rapidity up the swaying rope ladder and over the side.

To be honest, he had been watching for the pilot boat, not to see what to Sara Lee was the thrilling progress of the pilot up the ladder, but to get the newspapers he would bring on with him. It is perhaps explanatory of the way things went for Sara Lee from that time on that he quite forgot his newspapers.

The chairs were gone from the decks, preparatory to the morning landing, so they walked about and Sara Lee at last told him her story-the ladies of the Methodist Church, and the one hundred dollars a month she was to have, outside of her traveling expenses, to found and keep going a soup kitchen behind the lines.

"A hundred dollars a month," he said. "That's twenty pounds. Humph! Good God!"

But this last was under his breath.

Then she told him of Mabel Andrews' letter, and at last read it to him. He listened attentively. "Of course," she said when she had put the letter back into her bag, "I can't feed a lot, even with soup. But if I only help a few, it's worth doing, isn't it?"

"Very much worth doing," he said gravely. "I suppose you are not, by any chance, going to write a weekly article for one of your newspapers about what you are doing?"

"I hadn't thought of it. Do you think I should?"

Quite unexpectedly Mr. Travers patted her shoulder.

"My dear child," he said, "now and then I find somebody who helps to revive my faith in human nature. Thank you."

Sara Lee did not understand. The touch on the shoulder had made her think suddenly of Uncle James, and her chin quivered.

"I'm just a little frightened," she said in a small voice.

"Twenty pounds!" repeated Mr. Travers to himself. "Twenty pounds!" And aloud: "Of course you speak French?"

"Very little. I've had six lessons, and I can count-some."

The sense of unreality which the twenty pounds had roused in Mr. Travers' cautious British mind grew. No money, no French, no objective, just a great human desire to be useful in her own small way-this was a new type to him. What a sporting chance this frail bit of a girl was taking! And he noticed now something that had escaped him before —a dauntlessness, a courage of the spirit rather than of the body, that was in the very poise of her head.

"I'm not afraid about the language," she was saying. "I have a phrase book. And a hungry man, maybe sick or wounded, can understand a bowl of soup in any language, I should think. And I can cook!"

It was a perplexed and thoughtful Mr. Travers who sipped his Scotch-and-soda in the smoking room before retiring, he took the problem to bed with him and woke up in the night saying: "Twenty pounds! Good God!"

In the morning they left the ship. He found Sara Lee among the K's, waiting to have her passport examined, and asked her where she was stopping in London. She had read somewhere of Claridge's —in a novel probably.

"I shouldn't advise Claridge's," he said, reflecting rather grimly on the charges of that very exclusive hotel. "Suppose you let me make a suggestion."

So he wrote out the name of a fine old English house on Trafalgar Square, where she could stay until she went to France. There would be the matter of a passport to cross the Channel. It might take a day or two. Perhaps he could help her. He would give himself the pleasure of calling on her very soon.

Sara Lee got on the train and rode up to London. She said to herself over and over: "This is England. I am really in England." But it did not remove the sense of unreality. Even the English grass, bright green in midwinter, only added to the sense of unreality.

She tried, sitting in the strange train with its small compartments, to think of Harvey. She looked at her ring and tried to recall some of the tender things he had said to her. But Harvey eluded her. She could not hear his voice. And when she tried to see him it was Harvey of the wide face and the angry eyes of the last days that she saw.

Morley's comforted her. The man at the door had been there for forty years, and was beyond surprise. He had her story in twenty-four hours, and in forty-eight he was her slave. The elderly chambermaid mothered her, and failed to report that Sara Lee was doing a small washing in her room and had pasted handkerchiefs over the ancient walnut of her wardrobe.

"Going over, are you?" she said. "Dear me, what courage you've got, miss! They tell me things is horrible over there."

"That's why I'm going," replied Sara Lee, and insisted on helping to make up the bed.

"It's easier when two do it," she said casually.

Mr. Travers put in a fretful twenty-four hours before he came to see her. He lunched at Brooks', and astounded an elderly member of the House by putting her problem to him.

"A young girl!" exclaimed the M. P. "Why, deuce take it, it's no place for a young girl."

"An American," explained Mr. Travers uncomfortably. "She's perfectly able to look after herself."

"Probably a correspondent in disguise. They'll go to any lengths."

"She's not a correspondent."

"Let her stay in Boulogne. There's work there in the hospitals."

"She's not a nurse. She's a —well, she's a cook. Or so she says."

The M. P. stared at Mr. Travers, and Mr. Travers stared back defiantly.

"What in the name of God is she going to cook?"

"Soup," said Mr. Travers in a voice of suppressed irritation. "She's got a little money, and she wants to establish a soup kitchen behind the Belgian trenches on a line of communication. I suppose," he continued angrily, "even you will admit that the Belgian Army needs all the soup it can get."

"I don't approve of women near the lines."

"Neither do I. But I'm exceedingly glad that a few of them have the courage to go there."

"What's she going to make soup out of?"

"I'm not a cooking expert. But I know her and I fancy she'll manage."

It ended by the M. P. agreeing to use his influence with the War Office to get Sara Lee to France. He was very unwilling. The spy question was looming large those days. Even the Red Cross had unwittingly spread its protection over more than one German agent. The lines were being drawn in.

"I may possibly get her to France. I don't know, of course," he said in that ungracious tone in which an Englishman often grants a favor which he will go to any amount of trouble to do. "After that it's up to her."

Mr. Travers reflected rather grimly that after that it was apparently up to him.

Sara Lee sat in her room at Morley's Hotel and looked out at the life of London-policemen with chin straps; schoolboys in high silk hats and Eton suits, the hats generally in disreputable condition; clerks dressed as men at home dressed for Easter Sunday church; and men in uniforms. Only a fair sprinkling of these last, in those early days. On the first afternoon there was a military funeral. A regiment of Scots, in kilts, came swinging down from the church of St. Martin in the Fields, tall and wonderful men, grave and very sad. Behind them, on a gun carriage, was the body of their officer, with the British flag over the casket and his sword and cap on the top.

Sara Lee cried bitterly. It was not until they had gone that she remembered that Harvey had always called the Scots men in women's petticoats. She felt a thrill of shame for him, and no amount of looking at his picture seemed to help.

Mr. Travers called the second afternoon and was received by August at the door as an old friend.

"She's waiting in there," he said. "Very nice young lady, sir. Very kind to everybody."

Mr. Travers found her by a window looking out. There was a recruiting meeting going on in Trafalgar Square, the speakers standing on the monument. Now and then there was a cheer, and some young fellow sheepishly offered himself. Sara Lee was having a mad desire to go over and offer herself too. Because, she reflected, she had been in London almost two days, and she was as far from France as ever. Not knowing, of course, that three months was a fair time for the slow methods then in vogue.

There was a young man in the room, but Sara Lee had not noticed him. He was a tall, very blond young man, in a dark-blue Belgian uniform with a quaint cap which allowed a gilt tassel to drop over his forehead. He sat on a sofa, curling up the ends of a very small mustache, his legs, in cavalry boots, crossed and extending a surprising distance beyond the sofa.

The lights were up now, beyond the back drop, the stage darkened. A new scene with a vengeance, a scene laid in strange surroundings, with men, whole men and wounded men and spying men-and Sara Lee and this young Belgian, whose name was Henri and whose other name, because of what he suffered and what he did, we may not know.

IV

Henri sat on his sofa and watched Sara Lee. Also he shamelessly listened to the conversation, not because he meant to be an eavesdropper but because he liked Sara Lee's voice. He had expected a highly inflected British voice, and instead here was something entirely different-that is, Sara Lee's endeavor to reconcile the English "a" with her normal western Pennsylvania pronunciation. She did it quite unintentionally, but she had a good ear and it was difficult, for instance, to say "rather" when Mr. Travers said "rawther."

Henri had a good ear too. And the man he was waiting for did not come. Also he had been to school in England and spoke English rather better than most British. So he heard a conversation like this, the gaps being what he lost:

MR. TRAVERS: —— to France, anyhow. After that ——

SARA LEE: Awfully sorry to be —— But what shall I do if I do get over? The chambermaid up-stairs —— very difficult.

MR. TRAVERS: The proper and sensible thing is —— home.

SARA LEE: To America? But I haven't done anything yet.

Henri knew that she was an American. He also realized that she was on the verge of tears. He glared at poor Mr. Travers, who was doing his best, and lighted a French cigarette.

"There must be some way," said Sara Lee. "If they need help-and I have read you Mabel Andrews' letter-then I should think they'd be glad to send me."

"They would be, of course," he said. "But the fact is-there's been some trouble about spies, and —"

Henri's eyes narrowed.

"Spies! And they think I'm a spy?"

"My dear child," remonstrated Mr. Travers, slightly exasperated, "they're not thinking about you at all. The War Office has never heard of you. It's a general rule."

Sara Lee was not placated.

"Let them cable home and find out about me. I can give them references. Why, all sorts of prominent people are sending me money. They must trust me, or they wouldn't."

There were no gaps for Henri now. Sara Lee did not care who heard her, and even Mr. Travers had slightly raised his voice. Henri was divided between a conviction that he ought to go away and a mad desire to join in the conversation, greatly augmented when Sara Lee went to the window and wiped her eyes.

24

"If you only spoke French —" began Mr. Travers.

Sara Lee looked over her shoulder. "But of course I do!" she said. "And German and-and Yiddish, and all sorts of languages. Every spy does."

Henri smiled appreciatively.

It might all have ended there very easily. Sara Lee might have fought the War Office single-handed and won out, but it is extremely unlikely. The chances at that moment were that she would spend endless days and hours in anterooms, and tell her story and make her plea a hundred times. And then-go back home to Harvey and the Leete house, and after a time, like Mrs. Gregory, speak rather too often of "the time I went abroad."

But Sara Lee was to go to France, and even further, to the fragment of unconquered Belgium that remained. And never so long as she lived, would she be able to forget those days or to speak of them easily. So she stood by the window trying not to cry, and a little donkey drawing a coster's cart moved out in front of the traffic and was caught by a motor bus. There was only time for the picture-the tiny beast lying there and her owner wringing his hands. Such of the traffic as could get by swerved and went on. London must move, though a thousand willing little beasts lay dying.

And Sara moved too. One moment she was there by the window. And the next she had given a stifled cry and ran out.

"Bless my soul!" said Mr. Travers, and got up slowly.

Henri was already up and at the window. What he saw was Sara Lee making her way through the stream of vehicles, taking a dozen chances for her life. Henri waited until he saw her crouched by the donkey, its head on her knee. Then he, too, ran out.

That is how Henri, of no other name that may be given, met Sara Lee Kennedy, of Pennsylvania-under a London motor bus. And that, I think, will be the picture he carries of her until he dies, her soft eyes full of pity, utterly regardless of the dirt and the crowd and an expostulating bobby, with that grotesque and agonized head on her knees.

Henri crawled under the bus, though the policeman was extremely anxious to keep him out. And he ran a practiced eye over the injured donkey.

"It's dying," said Sara Lee with white lips.

"It will die," replied Henri, "but how soon? They are very strong, these little beasts."

The conductor of the bus made a suggestion then, one that froze the blood round Sara Lee's heart: "If you'll move away and let us run over it proper it'll be out of its trouble, miss."

Sara Lee raised haggard eyes to Henri.

"Did you hear that?" she said. "They'd do it too!"

The total result of a conference between four policemen, the costermonger, and, by that time, Mr. Travers-was to draw the animal off the street and into the square. Sara Lee stuck close by. So, naturally, did Henri. And when the hopeless condition of Nellie, as they learned she was named, became increasingly evident, Henri behaved like a man and a soldier.

He got out his revolver and shot her in the brain.

"A kindness," he explained, as Sara Lee would have caught his hand. "The only way, made-moiselle."

Mr. Travers had the usual British hatred of a crowd and publicity, coupled with a deadly fear of getting into the papers, except through an occasional letter to the *Times*. He vanished just before the shot, and might have been seen moving rapidly through the square, turning over in his mind the difficulty of trying to treat young American girls like rational human beings.

But Henri understood. He had had a French mother, and there is a leaven of French blood in the American temperament, old Huguenot, some of it. So Americans love beauty and obey their impulses and find life good to do things rather than to be something or other more or less important. And so Henri could quite understand how Sara Lee had forgotten herself when Mr. Travers could not. And he understood, also, when Sara Lee, having composed the little donkey's quiet figure, straightened up with tears in her eyes.

"It was very dear of you to come out," she said. "And-of course it was the best thing."

She held out her hand. The crowd had gone. Traffic was moving again, racing to make up for five lost precious moments. The square was dark, that first darkness of London, when air raids were threatened but had not yet taken place. From the top of the Admiralty, near by, a flashlight shot up into the air and began its nightly process of brushing the sky. Henri took her hand and bent over it.

"You are very brave, mademoiselle," he said, and touched her hand with his lips.

The amazing interlude had commenced.

V

Yet for a day or two nothing much was changed. Mr. Travers sent Sara Lee a note that he was taking up her problem with the Foreign Office; and he did indeed make an attempt. He also requested his wife to ask Sara Lee to tea.

Sara Lee was extremely nervous on the day she went. She wore a black jacket suit with a white collar, and she carried Aunt Harriet's mink furs, Aunt Harriet mourning thoroughly and completely in black astrachan. She had the faculty of the young American girl of looking smart without much expense, and she appeared absurdly young.

She followed the neat maid up a wide staircase to a door with a screen just inside, and heard her name announced for the first time in her life. Sara Lee took a long breath and went inside, to a most discouraging half hour.

Mr. Travers was on the hearth rug. Mrs. Travers was in a chair, a portly woman with a not unkindly face, but the brusque manner many Englishwomen acquire after forty. She held Sara Lee's hand and gave her a complete if smiling inspection.

"And it is you who are moving heaven and earth to get to the Front! You-child!"

Sara Lee's heart fell, but she smiled also.

"But I am older than I look," she said. "And I am very strong."

Mrs. Travers looked helplessly at her husband, while she rang the bell for tea. That was another thing Sara Lee had read about but never seen-that ringing for tea. At home no one served afternoon tea; but at a party, when refreshments were coming, the hostess slipped out to the kitchen and gave a whispered order or two.

"I shall be frank with you," said Mrs. Travers. "I think it quite impossible. It is not getting you over. That might be done. And of course there are women over there-young ones too. But the army objects very seriously to their being in danger. And of course one never knows —" Her voice trailed off vaguely. She implied, however, that what one never knows was best unknown.

"I have a niece over there," she said as the tea tray came in. "Her mother was fool enough to let her go. Now they can't get her back."

"Oh, dear!" said Sara Lee. "Can't they find her?"

"She won't come. Little idiot! She's in Paris, however. I daresay she is safe enough."

Mrs. Travers made the tea thoughtfully. So far Mr. Travers had hardly spoken, but he cheered in true British fashion at the sight of the tea. Sara Lee, exceedingly curious as to the purpose of a very small stand somewhat resembling a piano stool, which the maid had placed at her knee, learned that it was to hold her muffin plate.

"And now," said Mr. Travers, "suppose we come to the point. There doesn't seem to be a chance to get you over, my child. Same answer everywhere. Place is full of untrained women. Spies have been using Red Cross passes. Result is that all the lines are drawn as tight as possible."

Sara Lee stared at him with wide eyes.

"But I can't go back," she said. "I —well, I just can't. They're raising the money for me, and all sorts of people are giving things. A —a friend of mine is baking cakes and sending on the money. She has three children, and —"

She gulped.

"I thought everybody wanted to get help to the Belgians," she said.

A slightly grim smile showed itself on Mrs. Travers' face.

"I'm afraid you don't understand. It is you we want to help. Neither Mr. Travers nor I feel that a girl so young as you, and alone, has any place near the firing line. And that, I fancy, is where you wish to go. As to helping the Belgians, we have four in the house now. They do not belong to the same social circles, so they prefer tea in their own rooms. You are quite right about their needing help too. They cannot even make up their own beds."

"They are not all like that," broke in Mr. Travers hastily.

"Of course not. But I merely think that Miss-er-Kennedy should know both sides of the picture."

Somewhat later Sara Lee was ushered downstairs by the neat maid, who stood on the steps and blew a whistle for a taxi-Sara Lee had come in a bus. She carried in her hand the address of a Belgian commission of relief at the Savoy Hotel, and in her heart, for the first time, a doubt of her errand. She gave the Savoy address mechanically and, huddled in a corner, gave way to wild and fearful misgivings.

Coming up she had sat on top of the bus and watched with wide curious, eyes the strange traffic of London. The park had fascinated her-the little groups of drilling men in khaki, the mellow tones of a bugle, and here and there on the bridle paths well-groomed men and women on horseback, as clean-cut as the horses they rode, and on the surface as careless of what was happening across the Channel. But she saw nothing now. She sat back and twisted Harvey's ring on her finger, and saw herself going back, her work undone, her faith in herself shattered. And Harvey's arms and the Leete house ready to receive her.

However, a ray of hope opened for her at the Savoy-not much, a prospect.

The Savoy was crowded. Men in uniform, a sprinkling of anxious-faced wives and daughters, and more than a sprinkling of gaily dressed and painted women, filled the lobby or made their way slowly up and down the staircase. It was all so utterly different from what she had expected-so bright, so full of life. These well-fed people they seemed happy enough. Were they all wrong back home? Was the war the ghastly thing they thought it?

Long months afterward Sara Lee was to learn that the Savoy was not London. She was to learn other things-that America knew more, through a free press, of war conditions than did England. And she was to learn what never ceased to surprise her-the sporting instinct of the British which made their early slogan "Business as usual." Business and pleasure-but only on the surface. Underneath was a dogged and obstinate determination to make up as soon as possible for the humiliation of the early days of the war.

Those were the transition days in England. The people were slowly awaking to the magnitude of the thing that was happening to them. Certain elements of the press, long under political dominion, were preparing to come out for a coalition ministry. The question of high-explosive shells as against shrapnel was bitterly fought, some of the men at home standing fast for shrapnel, as valuable against German artillery as a garden hose. Men coming back from the Front were pleading for real help, not men only, not Red Cross, not food and supplies, but for something more competent than mere man power to hold back the deluge.

But over it all was that surface cheerfulness, that best-foot-forward attitude of London. And Sara Lee saw only that, and lost faith. She had come far to help. But here was food in plenty and bands playing and smiling men in uniform drinking tea and playing for a little. That, too, Sara Lee was to understand later; but just then she did not. At home there was more surface depression. The atrocities, the plight of the Belgians, the honor list in the *Illustrated London News* —that was the war to Sara Lee. And here!

But later on, down in a crowded dark little room, things were different. She was one of a long line, mostly women. They were unhappy and desolate enough, God knows. They sat or stood with a sort of weary resignation. Now and then a short heavy man with an upcurled mustache came out and took in one or two. The door closed. And overhead the band played monotonously.

It was after seven when Sara Lee's turn came. The heavy-set man spoke to her in French, but he failed to use a single one of the words she had memorized.

"Don't you speak any English?" she asked helplessly.

"I do; but not much," he replied. Though his French had been rapid he spoke English slowly. "How can we serve you, mademoiselle?"

"I don't want any assistance. I—I want to help, if I can."

"Here?"

"In France. Or Belgium."

He shrugged his shoulders.

"We have many offers of help. What we need, mademoiselle, is not workers. We have, at our base hospital, already many English nurses."

"I am not a nurse."

"I am sorry. The whole world is sorry for Belgium, and many would work. What we need" — he shrugged his shoulders again —"is food, clothing, supplies for our brave little soldiers."

Sara Lee looked extremely small and young. The Belgian sat down on a chair and surveyed her carefully.

"You English are doing a—a fine work for us," he observed. "We are grateful. But of course the" —he hesitated —"the pulling up of an entire people-it is colossal."

"But I am not English," said Sara Lee. "And I have a little money. I want to make soup for your wounded men at a railway station or-any place. I can make good soup. And I shall have money each month to buy what I need."

Only then was Sara Lee admitted to the crowded little room.

Long afterward, when the lights behind the back drop had gone down and Sara Lee was back again in her familiar setting, one of the clearest pictures she retained of that amazing interlude was of that crowded little room in the Savoy, its single littered desk, its two typewriters creating an incredible din, a large gentleman in a dark-blue military cape seeming to fill the room. And in corners and off stage, so to speak, perhaps a half dozen men, watching her curiously.

The conversation was in French, and Sara Lee's acquaintance of the passage acted as interpreter. It was only when Sara Lee found that a considerable discussion was going on in which she had no part that she looked round and saw her friend of two nights before and of the little donkey. He was watching her intently, and when he caught her eye he bowed.

Now men, in Sara Lee's mind, had until now been divided into the ones at home, one's own kind, the sort who married one's friends or oneself, the kind who called their wives "mother" after the first baby came, and were easily understood, plain men, decent and God-fearing and self-respecting; and the men of that world outside America, who were foreigners. One might like foreigners, but they were outsiders.

So there was no self-consciousness in Sara Lee's bow and smile. Later on Henri was to find that lack of self and sex consciousness one of the maddening mysteries about Sara Lee. Perhaps he never quite understood it. But always he respected it.

More conversation, in an increasing staccato. Short contributions from the men crowded into corners. Frenzied beating of the typewriting machines, and overhead and far away the band. There was no air in the room. Sara Lee was to find out a great deal later on about the contempt of the Belgians for air. She loosened Aunt Harriet's neckpiece.

So far Henri had not joined in the discussion. But now he came forward and spoke. Also, having finished, he interpreted to Sara Lee.

"They are most grateful," he explained. "It is a—a practical idea, mademoiselle. If you were in Belgium" —he smiled rather mirthlessly —"if you were already in the very small part of Belgium remaining to us, we could place you very usefully. But-the British War Office is most careful, just now. You understand-there are reasons."

Sara Lee flushed indignantly.

"They can watch me if they want to," she said. "What trouble can I make? I've only just landed. You-you'd have to go a good ways to find any one who knows less than I do about the war."

"There is no doubt of that," he said, unconscious of offense. "But the War Office —" He held out his hands.

Sara Lee, who had already caught the British "a" and was rather overdoing it, had a wild impulse to make the same gesture. It meant so much.

More conversation. Evidently more difficulties-but with Henri now holding the center of the stage and speaking rapidly. The heavy-set man retired and read letters under an electric lamp. The band upstairs was having dinner. And Henri argued and wrangled. He was quite passionate. The man in the military cape listened and smiled. And at last he nodded.

Henri turned to Sara Lee.

"You Americans are all brave," he said. "You like-what is it you say? —taking a chance, I think. Would you care to take such a chance?"

"What sort of a chance?"

"May I visit you this evening at your hotel?"

Just for an instant Sara Lee hesitated. There was Harvey at home. He would not like her receiving a call from any man. And Harvey did not like foreigners. He always said they had no respect for women. It struck her suddenly what Harvey would call Henri's bowing and his kissing her hand, and his passionate gesticulations when he was excited. He would call it all tomfool nonsense.

And she recalled his final words, his arms so close about her that she could hardly breathe, his voice husky with emotion.

"Just let me hear of any of those foreigners bothering you," he said, "and I'll go over and wipe out the whole damned nation."

It had not sounded funny then. It was not funny now.

"Please come," said Sara Lee in a small voice.

The other gentlemen bowed profoundly. Sara Lee, rather at a loss, gave them a friendly smile that included them all. And then she and Henri were walking up the stairs and to the entrance, Henri's tall figure the target for many women's eyes. He, however, saw no one but Sara Lee.

Henri, too, called a taxicab. Every one in London seemed to ride in taxis. And he bent over her hand, once she was in the car, but he did not kiss it.

"It is very kind of you, what you are doing," he said. "But, then, you Americans are all kind. And wonderful."

Back at Morley's Hotel Sara Lee had a short conversation with Harvey's picture.

"You are entirely wrong, dear," she said. She was brushing her hair at the time, and it is rather a pity that it was a profile picture and that Harvey's pictured eyes were looking off into space-that is, a piece of white canvas on a frame, used by photographers to reflect the light into the eyes. For Sara Lee with her hair down was even lovelier than with it up. "You were wrong. They are different, but they are kind and polite. And very, very respectful. And he is coming on business."

She intended at first to make no change in her frock. After all, it was not a social call, and if she did not dress it would put things on the right footing.

But slipping along the corridor after her bath, clad in a kimono and slippers and extremely nervous, she encountered a young woman on her way to dinner, and she was dressed in that combination of street skirt and evening blouse that some Englishwomen from the outlying districts still affect. And Sara Lee thereupon decided to dress. She called in the elderly maid, who was already her slave, and together they went over her clothes.

It was the maid, perhaps, then who brought into Sara Lee's life the strange and mad infatuation for her that was gradually to become a dominant issue in the next few months. For the maid chose a white dress, a soft and young affair in which Sara Lee looked like the heart of a rose.

"I always like to see a young lady in white, miss," said the maid. "Especially when there's a healthy skin."

So Sara Lee ate her dinner alone, such a dinner as a healthy skin and body demanded. And she watched tall young Englishwomen with fine shoulders go out with English officers in khaki, and listened to a babel of high English voices, and felt extremely alone and very subdued.

Henri came rather late. It was one of the things she was to learn about him later-that he was frequently late. It was only long afterward that she realized that such time as he spent with her was gained only at the cost of almost superhuman effort. But that was when she knew Henri's story, and his work. She waited for him in the reception room, where a man and a woman were having coffee and talking in a strange tongue. Henri found her there, at something before nine, rather downcast and worried, and debating about going up to bed. She looked up, to find him bowing before her.

"I thought you were not coming," she said.

"I? Not come? But I had said that I would come, mademoiselle. I may sit down?"

Sara Lee moved over on the velvet sofa, and Henri lowered his long body onto it. Lowered his voice, too, for the man and woman were staring at him.

"I'm afraid I didn't quite understand about this afternoon," began Sara Lee. "You spoke about taking a chance. I am not afraid of danger, if that is what you mean."

"That, and a little more, mademoiselle," said Henri. "But now that I am here I do not know."

His eyes were keen. Sara Lee had suddenly a strange feeling that he was watching the couple who talked over their coffee, and that, oddly enough, the couple were watching him. Yet he was apparently giving his undivided attention to her.

"Have you walked any to-day?" he asked her unexpectedly.

Sara Lee remembered the bus, and, with some bitterness, the two taxis.

"I haven't had a chance to walk," she said.

"But you should walk," he said. "I —will you walk with me? Just about the square, for air?" And in a lower tone: "It is not necessary that those two should know the plan, mademoiselle."

"I'll get my coat and hat," Sara Lee said, and proceeded to do so in a brisk and businesslike fashion. When she came down Henri was emerging from the telephone booth. His face was impassive. And again when in time Sara Lee was to know Henri's face better than she had ever known Harvey's, she was to learn that the masklike look he sometimes wore meant danger-for somebody.

They went out without further speech into the clear cold night. Henri, as if from custom, threw his head back and scanned the sky. Then they went on and crossed into the square.

"The plan," Henri began abruptly, "is this: You will be provided to-morrow with a passport to Boulogne. You will, if you agree, take the midnight train for Folkestone. At the railway station here you will be searched. At Folkestone a board, sitting in an office on the quay, will examine your passport."

"Does any one in Boulogne speak English?" Sara Lee inquired nervously. Somehow that babel of French at the Savoy had frightened her. Her little phrase book seemed pitifully inadequate for the great things in her mind.

"That hardly matters," said Henri, smiling faintly. "Because I think you shall not go to Boulogne."

"Not go!" She stopped dead, under the monument, and looked up at him.

"The place for you to go, to start from, is Calais," Henri explained. He paused, to let pass two lovers, a man in khaki and a girl. "But Calais is difficult. It is under martial law —a closed city. From Boulogne to Calais would be perhaps impossible."

Sara Lee was American and her methods were direct.

"How can I get to Calais?"

"Will you take the chance I spoke of?"

"For goodness' sake," said Sara Lee in an exasperated tone, "how can I tell you until I know what it is?"

30

Henri told her. He even, standing under a street lamp, drew a small sketch for her, to make it clear. Sara Lee stood close, watching him, and some of the lines were not as steady as they might have been. And in the midst of it he suddenly stopped.

"Do you know what it means?" he demanded.

"Yes, of course."

"And you know what date this is?"

"The eighteenth of February."

But he saw, after all, that she did not entirely understand.

"To-night, this eighteenth of February, the Germans commence a blockade of this coast. No vessels, if they can prevent them, will leave the harbors; or if they do, none shall reach the other side!"

"Oh!" said Sara Lee blankly.

"We are eager to do as you wish, mademoiselle. But" —he commenced slowly to tear up the sketch —"it is too dangerous. You are too young. If anything should go wrong and I had-No. We will find another way."

He put the fragments of the sketch in his pocket.

"How long is this blockade to last?" Sara Lee asked out of bitter disappointment.

He shrugged his shoulders.

"Who can say? A week! A year! Not at all!"

"Then," said Sara Lee with calm deliberation, "you might as well get out your pencil and draw another picture-because I'm going."

Far enough away now, the little house at home and the peace that dwelt therein; and Harvey; and the small white bedroom; and the daily round of quiet duties. Sara Lee had set her face toward the east, and the land of dying men. And as Henri looked down at her she had again that poised and eager look, almost of flight, that had brought into Harvey's love for her just a touch of fear.

VI

Sara Lee Kennedy was up at dawn the next morning. There was a very serious matter to decide, for Henri's plan had included only such hand luggage as she herself could carry.

Sara Lee carefully laid out on the bed such articles as she could not possibly do without, and was able to pack into her suitcase less than a fourth of them. She had fortunately brought a soft wool sweater, which required little room. Undergarments, several blouses, the sweater and a pair of heavy shoes-that was her equipment, plus such small toilet outfit as is necessary when a young woman uses no make-up and regards cold cream only as a remedy for chapped hands.

The maid found her in rather a dismal mood.

"Going across, miss!" she said. "Fancy that!"

"It's a secret," cautioned Sara Lee. "I am really not sure I am going. I am only trying to go."

The maid, who found Sara Lee and the picture of Harvey on her dressing table both romantic and appealing, offered to pack. From the first moment it was evident that she meant to include the white dress. Indeed she packed it first.

"You never know what's going to happen over there," she asserted. "They do say that royalties are everywhere, going about like common people. You'd better have a good frock with you."

She had an air of subdued excitement, and after she had established the fact that not only the white frock but slippers and hose also would go in she went to the door and glanced up and down the passage. Then she closed the door.

"There was queer goings-on here last night, miss," she said cautiously. "Spies!"

"Oh, no!" cried Sara Lee.

"Spies," she repeated. "A man and a woman, pretending to be Belgian refugees. They took them away at daylight. I expect by now they've been shot."

Sara Lee ate very little breakfast that morning. All through England it was confidently believed that spies were shot on discovery, a theory that has been persistent-and false, save at the battle line-since the beginning of the war. And Henri's plan assumed new proportions. Suppose she made her attempt and failed? Suppose they took her for a spy, and that tomorrow's sun found her facing a firing squad? Not, indeed, that she had ever heard of a firing squad, as such. But she had seen spies shot in the movies. They invariably stood in front of a brick wall, with the hero in the center.

So she absent-mindedly ate her kippered herring, which had been strongly recommended by the waiter, and tried to think of what a spy would do, so she might avoid any suspicious movements. It struck her, too, that war seemed to have made the people on that side of the ocean extremely ready with weapons. They would be quite likely to shoot first and ask questions afterwards-which would be too late to be helpful.

She remembered Henri, for instance, and the way, without a word, he had shot the donkey. That day she wrote Harvey a letter.

> *"Dearest:"* it began; "I think I am to leave for France to-night. Things seem to
> be moving nicely, and I am being helped by the Belgian Relief Commission. It
> is composed of Belgians and is at the Savoy Hotel."

Here she stopped and cried a little. What if she should never see Harvey again-never have his sturdy arms about her? Harvey gained by distance. She remembered only his unfailing kindness and strength and his love for her. He seemed, here at the edge of the whirlpool, a sort of eddy of peace and quiet. Even then she had no thought of going back until her work was done, but she did an unusual thing for her, unused to demonstration of any sort. She kissed his ring.

Followed directions about sending the money from the church society, a description of Morley's and Trafalgar Square, an account of tea at the Travers', and of the little donkey-without mention, however, of Henri. She felt that Harvey would not understand Henri.

But at the end came the passage which poor Harvey read and re-read when the letter came, and alternately ground his teeth over and kissed.

> "I do love you, Harvey dear. And I am coming back to you. I have felt that I
> had to do what I am doing, but I am coming back. That's a promise. Unless,
> of course, I should take sick, or something like that, which isn't likely."

There was a long pause in the writing here, but Harvey could not know that.

> "I shall wear your ring always; and always, Harvey, it will mean to me that I
> belong to you. With dearest love.

> "SARA LEE"

Then she added a postscript, of course.

> "The War Office is not letting people cross to Calais just now. But I am going
> to do it anyhow. It is perfectly simple. And when I get over I shall write and
> tell you how.

> "S.L."

It was the next day that an indignant official in the censor's office read that postscript, and rose in his wrath and sent a third Undersomething-or-other to look up Sara Lee at Morley's. But by this time she was embarked on the big adventure; and by the time a cable reached Calais there was no trace of Sara Lee.

During the afternoon she called up Mr. Travers at his office, and rather gathered that he did not care to use the telephone during business hours.

"I just wanted to tell you that you need not bother about me any more," she said. "I am being sent over and I think everything is all right."

He was greatly relieved. Mrs. Travers had not fully indorsed his encomiums of the girl. She had felt that no really nice girl would travel so far on so precarious an errand, particularly when she was alone. And how could one tell, coming from America, how her sympathies really lay? She might be of German parentage-the very worst sort, because they spoke American. It was easy enough to change a name.

Nevertheless, Mr. Travers felt a trifle low in his mind when he hung up the receiver. He said twice to himself: "Twenty pounds!" And at last he put four sovereigns in an envelope and sent them to her anonymously by messenger. Sara Lee guessed whence they came, but she respected the manner of the gift and did not thank him. It was almost the first gold money she had ever seen.

She was very carefully searched at the railway station that night and found that her American Red Cross button, which had come with her dollar subscription to the association, made the matron inspector rather kindly inclined. Nevertheless, she took off Sara Lee's shoes, and ran over the lining of her coat, and quite ruined the maid's packing of the suitcase.

"You are going to Boulogne?" asked the matron inspector.

Sara Lee did not like to lie.

"Wherever the boat takes me," she said with smile.

The matron smiled too.

"I shouldn't be nervous, miss," she said. "It's a chance, of course, but they have not done much damage yet."

It was after midnight then, and a cold fog made the station a gloomy thing of blurred yellow lights and raw chill. A few people moved about, mostly officers in uniform. Half a dozen men in civilian clothes eyed her as she passed through the gates; Scotland Yard, but she did not know. And once she thought she saw Henri, but he walked away into the shadows and disappeared. The train, looking as absurdly small and light as all English trains do, was waiting out in the shed. There were no porters, and Sara Lee carried her own bag.

She felt quite sure she had been mistaken about Henri, for of course he would have come and carried it for her.

The train was cold and quiet. When it finally moved out it was under way before she knew that it was going. And then suddenly Sara Lee's heart began to pound hard.

It was a very cold and shivering Sara Lee who curled up, alone in her compartment, and stared hard at Harvey's ring to keep her courage up. But a curious thing had happened. Harvey gave her no moral support. He brought her only disapproval. She found herself remembering none of the loving things he had said to her, but only the bitter ones.

Perhaps it was the best thing for her, after all. For a sort of dogged determination to go through with it all, at any cost, braced her to her final effort.

So far it had all been busy enough, but not comfortable. She was cold, and she had eaten almost nothing all day. As the hours went on and the train slid through the darkness she realized that she was rather faint. The steam pipes, only warm at the start, were entirely cold by one o'clock, and by two Sara Lee was sitting on her feet, with a heavy coat wrapped about her knees.

The train moved quietly, as do all English trains, with no jars and little sound. There were few lights outside, for the towns of Eastern England were darkened, like London, against air attacks. So when she looked at the window she saw only her own reflection, white and wide-eyed, above Aunt Harriet's fur neckpiece.

In the next compartment an officer was snoring, but she did not close her eyes. Perhaps, for that last hour, some of the glow that had brought her so far failed her. She was not able to think beyond Folkestone, save occasionally, and that with a feeling that it should not be made so difficult to do a kind and helpful thing.

At a quarter before three the train eased down. In the same proportion Sara Lee's pulse went up. A long period of crawling along, a stop or two, but no resultant opening of the doors; and at last, in a cold rain and a howling wind from the channel, the little seaport city.

More officers than she had suspected, a few women, got out. The latter Sara Lee's experience on the steamer enabled her to place; buyers mostly, and Americans, on their way to Paris, blockade or no blockade, because the American woman must be well and smartly gowned and hatted. A man with a mourning band on his sleeve carried a wailing child.

The officers lighted cigarettes. The civilians formed a line on the jetty under the roof of the shed, and waited, passports in hand, before a door that gleamed with yellow light. Faces looked pale and anxious. The blockade was on, and Germany had said that no ships would cross that night.

As if defiantly the Boulogne boat, near at hand, was ablaze, on the shore side at least, with lights. Stewards came and went. Beyond it lay the harbor, dark and mysterious save where, from somewhere across, a flashlight made a brave effort to pierce the fog.

One of the buyers ahead of Sara Lee seemed exhilarated by the danger ahead.

"They'll never get us," she said. "Look at that fog!"

"It's lifting, dearie," answered a weary voice behind her. "The wind is carrying it away."

When Sara Lee's turn came she was ready. A group of men in civilian clothes, seated about a long table, looked her over carefully. Her passports moved deliberately from hand to hand. A long business, and the baby wailing harder than ever. But the office was at least warm. Some of her failing courage came back as she moved, following her papers, round the table. They were given back to her at last, and she went out. She had passed the first ordeal.

Suitcase in hand she wandered down the stone jetty. The Boulogne boat she passed, and kept on. At the very end, dark and sinister, lay another boat. It had no lights. The tide was in, and its deck lay almost flush with the pier. Sara Lee walked on toward it until a voice spoke to her out of the darkness and near at hand.

"Your boat is back there, madam."

"I know. Thank you. I am just walking about."

The petty officer-he was a petty officer, though Sara Lee had never heard the term-was inclined to be suspicious. Under excuse of lighting his pipe he struck a match, and Sara Lee's young figure stood out in full relief. His suspicions died away with the flare.

"Bad night, miss," he offered.

"Very," said Sara Lee, and turned back again.

This time, bewildered and uneasy, she certainly saw Henri. But he ignored her. He was alone, and smoking one of his interminable cigarettes. He had not said he was crossing, and why had he not spoken to her? He wandered past down the pier, and she lost him in the shadows. When he came back he paused near her, and at last saluted and spoke.

"*Pardon*," he said. "If you will stand back here you will find less wind."

"Thank you."

He carried her suitcase back, and stooping over to place it at her feet he said: "I shall send him on board with a message to the captain. When I come back try again."

He left her at once. The passengers for Boulogne were embarking now. A silent lot, they disappeared into the warmth and brightness of the little boat and were lost. No one paid any attention to Sara Lee standing in the shadows.

Soon Henri came back. He walked briskly and touched his cap as he passed. He went aboard the Boulogne steamer, and without a backward glance disappeared.

Sara Lee watched him out of sight, in a very real panic. He had been something real and tangible in that shadowy place-something familiar in an unfamiliar world. But he was gone. She threw up her head.

So once more Sara Lee picked up her suitcase and went down the pier. Now she was unchallenged. What lurking figure might be on the dark deck of the Calais boat she could not tell. That was the chance she was to take. The gangway was still out, and as quietly as possible she went aboard. The Boulogne boat had suddenly gone dark, and she heard the churning of the screw. With the extinction of the lights on the other boat came at last deeper night to her aid. A few steps, a stumble, a gasp-and she was on board the forbidden ship.

She turned forward, according to her instructions, where the overhead deck made below an even deeper shadow. Henri had said that there were cabins there, and that the chance was of finding an unlocked one. If they were all locked she would be discovered at dawn, and arrested. And Sara Lee was not a war correspondent. She was not accustomed to arrest. Indeed she had a deep conviction that arrest in her case would mean death. False, of course, but surely it shows her courage.

As she stood there, breathless and listening, the Boulogne boat moved out. She heard the wash against the jetty, felt the rolling of its waves. But being on the landward side she could not see the faint gleam of a cigarette that marked Henri's anxious figure at the rail. So long as the black hulk of the Calais boat was visible, and long after indeed, Henri stood there, outwardly calm but actually shaken by many fears. She had looked so small and young; and who could know what deviltry lurked abroad that night?

He had not gone with her because it was necessary that he be in Boulogne the next morning. And also, the very chance of getting her across lay in her being alone and unobserved.

So he stood by the rail and looked back and said a wordless little prayer that if there was trouble it come to his boat and not to the other. Which might very considerably have disturbed the buyers had they known of it and believed in prayer.

Sara Lee stood in the shadows and listened. There were voices overhead, from the bridge. A door opened onto the deck and threw out a ray of light. Some one came out and went on shore, walking with brisk ringing steps. And then at last she put down her bag and tried door after door, without result.

The man who had gone ashore called another. The gangway was drawn in. The engines began to vibrate under foot. Sara Lee, breathless and terrified, stood close to a cabin door and remained immovable. At one moment it seemed as if a seaman was coming forward to where she stood. But he did not come.

The Calais boat was waiting until the other steamer had got well out of the harbor. The fog had lifted, and the searchlight was moving over the surface. It played round the channel steamer without touching it. But none of this was visible to Sara Lee.

At last the lights of the quay began to recede. The little boat rocked slightly in its own waves as it edged away. It moved slowly through the shipping and out until, catching the swell of the channel, it shot ahead at top speed.

For an hour Sara Lee stood there. The channel wind caught her and tore at her skirts until she was almost frozen. And finally, in sheer desperation, she worked her way round to the other side. She saw no one. Save for the beating heart of the engine below it might have been a dead ship.

On the other side she found an open door and stumbled into the tiny dark deck cabin, as chilled and frightened a philanthropist as had ever crossed that old and tricky and soured bit of seaway. And there, to be frank, she forgot her fright in as bitter a tribute of seasickness as even the channel has ever exacted.

She had locked herself in, and she fell at last into an exhausted sleep. When she wakened and peered out through the tiny window it was gray winter dawn. The boat was quiet, and before her lay the quay of Calais and the Gare Maritime. A gangway was out and a hurried survey showed no one in sight.

Sara Lee picked up her suitcase and opened the door. The fresh morning air revived her, but nevertheless it was an extremely pale young woman who, obeying Henri's instructions, went ashore that morning in the gray dawn unseen, undisturbed and unquestioned. But from the moment she appeared on the gangway until the double glass doors of the Gare Maritime closed behind her this apparently calm young woman did not breathe at all. She arrived, indeed, with lungs fairly collapsed and her heart entirely unreliable.

A woman clerk was asleep at a desk. Sara Lee roused her to half wakefulness, no interest and extremely poor English. A drowsy porter led her up a staircase and down an endless corridor. Then at last he was gone, and Sara Lee turned the key in her door and burst into tears.

VII

Now up to this point Sara Lee's mind had come to rest at Calais. She must get there; after that the other things would need to be worried over. Henri had already in their short acquaintance installed himself as the central figure of this strange and amazing interlude-not as a good-looking young soldier surprisingly fertile in expedients, but as a sort of agent of providence, by whom and through whom things were done.

And Henri had said she was to go to the Gare Maritime at Calais and make herself comfortable-if she got there. After that things would be arranged.

Sara Lee therefore took a hot bath, though hardly a satisfactory one, for there was no soap and she had brought none. She learned later on to carry soap with her everywhere. So she soaked the chill out of her slim body and then dressed. The room was cold, but a great exultation kept her warm. She had run the blockade, she had escaped the War Office-which, by the way, was looking her up almost violently by that time, via the censor. It had found the trunk she left at Morley's, and cross-questioned the maid into hysteria-and here she was, safe in France, the harbor of Calais before her, and here and there strange-looking war craft taking on coal. Destroyers, she learned later. Her ignorance was rather appalling at first.

It was all unreal-the room with its cold steam pipes, the heavy window hangings, the very words on the hot and cold taps in the bathroom. A great vessel moved into the harbor. As it turned she saw its name printed on its side in huge letters, and the flag, also painted, of a neutral country —a hoped-for protection against German submarines. It brought home to her, rather, the thing she had escaped.

After a time she thought of food, but rather hopelessly. Her attempts to get *savon* from a stupid boy had produced nothing more useful than a flow of unintelligible French and no soap whatever. She tried a pantomime of washing her hands, but to the boy she had appeared to be merely wringing them. And, as a great many females were wringing their hands in France those days, he had gone away, rather sorry for her.

When hunger drove her to the bell again he came back and found her with her little phrase book in her hands, feverishly turning the pages. She could find plenty of sentences such as "*Garçon, vous avez renversé du vin sur ma robe*," but not an egg lifted its shining pate above the pages. Not cereal. Not fruit. Not even the word breakfast.

Long, long afterward Sara Lee found a quite delightful breakfast hidden between two pages that were stuck together. But it was then far too late.

"*Donnez-moi*," began Sara Lee, and turned the pages rapidly, "this; do you see?" She had found roast beef.

The boy observed stolidly, in French, that it was not ready until noon. She was able to make out, from his failing to depart, that there was no roast beef.

"Good gracious!" she said, ravenous and exasperated. "Go and get me some bread and coffee, anyhow." She repeated it, slightly louder.

That was the tableau that Henri found when, after a custom that may be war or may be Continental, he had inquired the number of her room and made his way there.

There was a twinkle in his blue eyes as he bowed before her-and a vast relief too.

"So you are here!" he said in a tone of satisfaction. He had put in an extremely bad night, even for him, by whom nights were seldom wasted in a bed. While he was with her something of her poise had communicated itself to him. He had felt the confidence, in men and affairs, that American girls are given as a birthright. And her desire for service he had understood as a year or two ago he could not have understood. But he had stood by the rail staring north, and cursing himself for having placed her in danger during the entire crossing.

There was nothing about him that morning, however to show his bad hours. He was debonnaire and smiling.

"I am famishing," said Sara Lee. "And there are no eggs in this book-none whatever."

"Eggs! You wish eggs?"

"I just want food. Almost anything will do. I asked for eggs because they can come quickly."

Henri turned to the boy and sent him off with a rapid order. Then: "May I come in?" he said.

Sara Lee cast an uneasy glance over the room. It was extremely tidy, and unmistakably it was a bedroom. But though her color rose she asked him in. After all, what did it matter? To have refused would have looked priggish, she said to herself. And as a matter of fact one of the early lessons she learned in France was learned that morning-that though convention had had to go, like many other things in the war, men who were gentlemen ignored its passing.

Henri came in and stood by the center table.

"Now, please tell me," he said. "I have been most uneasy. On the quay last night you looked-frightened."

"I was awfully frightened. Nothing happened. I even slept."

"You were very brave."

"I was very seasick."

"I am sorry."

Henri took a turn up and down the room.

"But," said Sara Lee slowly, "I —I —can't be on your hands, you know. You must have many things to do. If you are going to have to order my meals and all that, I'm going to be a dreadful burden."

"But you will learn very quickly."

"I'm stupid about languages."

Henri dismissed that with a gesture. She could not, he felt, be stupid about anything. He went to the window and looked out. The destroyers were still coaling, and a small cargo was being taken off the boat at the quay. The rain was over, and in the early sunlight an officer in blue tunic, red breeches and black cavalry boots was taking the air, his head bent over his chest. Not a detail of the scene escaped him.

"I have agreed to find the right place for you," he said thoughtfully. "There is one, but I think —" He hesitated. "I do not wish to place you again in danger."

"You mean that it is near the Front?"

"Very near, mademoiselle."

"But I should be rather near, to be useful."

"Perhaps, for your work. But what of you? These brutes-they shell far and wide. One can never be sure."

He paused and surveyed her whimsically.

"Who allowed you to come, alone, like this?" he demanded. "Is there no one who objected?"

Sara Lee glanced down at her ring.

"The man I am going to marry. He is very angry."

Henri looked at her, and followed her eyes to Harvey's ring. He said nothing, however, but he went over and gave the bell cord a violent jerk.

"You must have food quickly," he said in a rather flat voice. "You are looking tired and pale."

A sense of unreality was growing on Sara Lee. That she should be alone in France with a man she had never seen three days before; that she knew nothing whatever about that man; that, for the present at least, she was utterly and absolutely dependent on him, even for the food she ate-it was all of a piece with the night's voyage and the little room at the Savoy. And it was none of it real.

When the breakfast tray came Henri was again at the window and silent. And Sara Lee saw that it was laid for two. She was a little startled, but the businesslike way in which the young officer drew up two chairs and held one out for her made protest seem absurd. And the flat-faced boy, who waited, looked unshocked and uninterested.

It was not until she had had some coffee that Henri followed up his line of thought.

"So-the fiance did not approve? It is not difficult to understand. There is always danger, for there are German aëroplanes even in remote places. And you are very young. You still wish to establish yourself, mademoiselle?"

"Of course!"

"Would it be a comfort to cable your safe arrival in France to the fiancé?" When he saw her face he smiled. And if it was a rather heroic smile it was none the less friendly. "I see. What shall I say? Or will you write it?"

So Sara Lee, vastly cheered by two cups of coffee, an egg, and a very considerable portion of bread and butter, wrote her cable. It was to be brief, for cables cost money. It said, "Safe. Well. Love." And Henri, who seemed to have strange and ominous powers, sent it almost immediately. Total cost, as reported to Sara Lee, two francs. He took the money she offered him gravely.

"We shall cable quite often," he said. "He will be anxious. And I think he has a right to know."

The "we" was entirely unconscious.

"And now," he said, when he had gravely allowed Sara Lee to pay her half of the breakfast, "we must arrange to get you out of Calais. And that, mademoiselle, may take time."

It took time. Sara Lee, growing accustomed now to little rooms entirely filled with men and typewriters, went from one office to another, walking along the narrow pavements with Henri, through streets filled with soldiers. Once they drew aside to let pass a procession of Belgian refugees, those who had held to their village homes until bombardment had destroyed them-stout peasant women in short skirts and with huge bundles, old men, a few young ones, many children. The terror of the early flight was not theirs, but there was in all of them a sort of sodden hopelessness that cut Sara Lee to the heart. In an irregular column they walked along, staring ahead but seeing nothing. Even the children looked old and tired.

Sara Lee's eyes filled with tears.

"My people," said Henri. "Simple country folk, and going to England, where they will grieve for the things that are gone-their fields and their sons. The old ones will die, quickly, of homesickness. It is difficult to transplant an old tree."

The final formalities seemed to offer certain difficulties. Henri, who liked to do things quickly and like a prince, flushed with irritation. He drew himself up rather haughtily in reply to one question, and glanced uneasily at the girl. But it was all as intelligible as Sanskrit to her.

It was only after a whispered sentence to the man at the head of the table that the paper was finally signed.

As they went down to the street together Sara Lee made a little protest.

"But I simply must not take all your time," she said, looking up anxiously. "I begin to realize how foolhardy the whole thing is. I meant well, but-it is you who are doing everything; not I."

"I shall not make the soup, mademoiselle," he replied gravely.

VIII

Here were more things to do. Sara Lee's money must be exchanged at a bank for French gold. She had three hundred dollars, and it had been given her in a tiny brown canvas bag. And then there was the matter of going from Calais toward the Front. She had expected to find a train, but there were no trains. All cars were being used for troops. She stared at Henri in blank dismay.

"No trains!" she said blankly. "Would an automobile be very expensive?"

"They are all under government control, mademoiselle. Even the petrol."

She stopped in the street.

"Then I shall have to go back."

Henri laughed boyishly.

"Mademoiselle," he said, "I have been requested to take you to a place where you may render us the service we so badly need. For the present that is my duty, and nothing else. So if you will accept the offer of my car, which is a shameful one but travels well, we can continue our journey."

Long, long afterward, Sara Lee found a snapshot of Henri's car, taken by a light-hearted British officer. Found it and sat for a long time with it in her hand, thinking and remembering that first day she saw it, in the sun at Calais. A long low car it was, once green, but now roughly painted gray. But it was not the crude painting, significant as it was, that brought so close the thing she was going to. It was that the car was but a shell of a car. The mud guards were crumpled up against the side. Body and hood were pitted with shrapnel. A door had been shot away, and the wind shield was but a frame set round with broken glass. Even the soldier-chauffeur wore a patch over one eye, and his uniform was ragged.

"Not a beautiful car, mademoiselle, as I warned you! But a fast one!"

Henri was having a double enjoyment. He was watching Sara Lee's face and his chauffeur's remaining eye.

"But fast; eh, Jean?" he said to the chauffeur. The man nodded and said something in French. It was probably the thing Henri had hoped for, and he threw back his head and laughed.

"Jean is reminding me," he said gayly, "that it is forbidden to officers to take a lady along the road that we shall travel." But when he saw how Sara Lee flushed he turned to the man.

"Mademoiselle has come from America to help us, Jean," he said quietly. "And now for Dunkirk."

The road from Dunkirk to Calais was well guarded in those days. From Nieuport for some miles inland only the shattered remnant of the Belgian Army held the line. For the cry "On to Paris!" the Germans had substituted "On to Calais!"

So, on French soil at least, the road was well guarded. A few miles in the battered car, then a slowing up, a showing of passports, the clatter of a great chain as it dropped to the road, a lowering of leveled rifles, and a salute from the officer-that was the method by which they advanced.

Henri sat with the driver and talked in a low tone. Sometimes he sat quiet, looking ahead. He seemed, somehow, older, more careworn. His boyishness had gone. Now and then he turned to ask if she was comfortable, but in the intervals she felt that he had entirely forgotten her. Once, at something Jean said, he got out a pocket map and went over it carefully. It was a long time after that before he turned to see if she was all right.

Sara Lee sat forward and watched everything. She saw little evidence of war, beyond the occasional sentries and chains. Women were walking along the roads. Children stopped and pointed, smiling, at the battered car. One very small boy saluted, and Henri as gravely returned the salute.

Some time after that he turned to her.

"I find that I shall have to leave you in Dunkirk," he said. "A matter of a day only, probably. But I will see before I go that you are comfortable."

"I shall be quite all right, of course."

But something had gone out of the day for her.

Sara Lee learned one thing that day, learned it as some women do learn, by the glance of an eye, the tone of a voice. The chauffeur adored Henri. His one unbandaged eye stole moments from the road to glance at him. When he spoke, while Henri read his map, his very voice betrayed him. And while she pondered the thing, woman-fashion they drew into the square of Dunkirk, where the statue of Jean Bart, pirate and privateer stared down at this new procession of war which passed daily and nightly under his cold eyes.

Jean and a porter carried in her luggage. Henri and a voluble and smiling Frenchwoman showed her to her room. She felt like an island of silence in a rapid-rolling sea of French. The Frenchwoman threw open the door.

A great room with high curtained windows; a huge bed with a faded gilt canopy and heavy draperies; a wardrobe as vast as the bed; and for a toilet table an enormous mirror reaching to the ceiling and with a marble shelf below-that was her room.

"I think you will be comfortable here, mademoiselle."

Sara Lee, who still clutched her small bag of gold, shook her head.

"Comfortable, yes," she said. "But I am afraid it is very expensive."

Henri named an extremely low figure-an exact fourth, to be accurate, of its real cost. A surprising person Henri, with his worn uniform and his capacity for kindly mendacity. And seeing something in the Frenchwoman's face that perhaps he had expected, he turned to her almost fiercely:

"You are to understand, madame, that this lady has been placed in my care by authority that will not be questioned. She is to have every deference."

That was all, but was enough. And from that time on Sara Lee Kennedy, of Ohio, was called, in the tiny box downstairs which constituted the office, "Mademoiselle La Princesse."

Henri did a characteristic and kindly thing for Sara Lee before he left that evening on one of the many mysterious journeys that he was to make during the time Sara Lee knew him. He came to her door, menus in hand, and painstakingly ordered for her a dinner for that night, and the three meals for the day following.

He made no suggestion of dining with her that evening. Indeed, watching him from her small table, Sara Lee decided that he had put her entirely out of his mind. He did not so much as glance at her. Save the cashier at her boxed-in desk and money drawer, she was the only woman in that room full of officers. Quite certainly Henri was the only man who did not find some excuse for glancing in her direction.

But finishing early, he paused by the cashier's desk to pay for his meal, and then he gave Sara Lee the stiffest and most ceremonious of bows.

She felt hurt. Alone in her great room, the curtains drawn by order of the police, lest a ray of light betray the town to eyes in the air, she went carefully over the hours she had spent with Henri that day, looking for a cause of offense. She must have hurt him or he would surely have stopped to speak to her.

Perhaps already he was finding her a burden. She flushed with shame when she remembered about the meals he had had to order for her, and she sat up in her great bed until late, studying by candlelight such phrases as:

"Il y a une erreur dans la note," and *"Garçon, quels fruits avez-vous?"*

She tried to write to Harvey that night, but she gave it up at last. There was too much he would not understand. She could not write frankly without telling of Henri, and to this point everything had centered about Henri. It all rather worried her, because there was nothing she was ashamed of, nothing she should have had to conceal. She had yet to learn, had Sara Lee, that many of the concealments of life are based not on wrongdoing but on fear of misunderstanding.

So she got as far as: *"Dearest Harvey*: I am here in a hotel at Dunkirk"* —and then stopped, fairly engulfed in a wave of homesickness. Not so much for Harvey as for familiar things-Uncle James in his chair by the fire, with the phonograph playing "My Little Gray Home in the West"; her own white bedroom; the sun on the red geraniums in the dining-room window; the voices of happy children wandering home from school.

She got up and went to the window, first blowing out the candle. Outside, the town lay asleep, and from a gate in the old wall a sentry with a bugle blew a quiet "All's well." From somewhere near, on top of the *mairie* perhaps, where eyes all night searched the sky for danger, came the same trumpet call of safety for the time, of a little longer for quiet sleep.

For two days the girl was alone. There was no sign of Henri. She had nothing to read, and her eyes, watching hour after hour the panorama that passed through the square under her window, searched vainly for his battered gray car. In daytime the panorama was chiefly of motor lorries-she called them trucks-piled high with supplies, often fodder for the horses in that vague district beyond ammunition and food. Now and then a battery rumbled through, its gunners on the limbers, detached, with folded arms; and always there were soldiers.

Sometimes, from her window, she saw the market people below, in their striped red-and-white booths, staring up at the sky. She would look up, too, and there would be an aëroplane sliding along, sometimes so low that one could hear the faint report of the exhaust.

But it was the ambulances that Sara Lee looked for. Mostly they came at night, a steady stream of them. Sometimes they moved rapidly. Again, one would be going very slowly, and other machines would circle impatiently round it and go on. A silent, grim procession in the moonlight it was, and it helped the girl to bear the solitude of those two interminable days.

Inside those long gray cars with the red crosses painted on the tops —a symbol of mercy that had ceased to protect-inside those cars were wounded men, men who had perhaps lain for hours without food or care. Surely, surely it was right that she had come. The little she could do must count in the great total. She twisted Harvey's ring on her finger and sent a little message to him.

"You will forgive me when you know, dear," was the message. "It is so terrible! So pitiful!"

Yet during the day the square was gay enough. Officers in spurs clanked across, wide capes blowing in the wind. Common soldiers bought fruit and paper bags of fried potatoes from the booths. Countless dogs fought under the feet of passers-by, and over all leered the sardonic face of Jean Bart, pirate and privateer.

Sara Lee went out daily, but never far. And she practiced French with the maid, after this fashion:

"*Draps de toile*," said the smiling maid, putting the linen sheets on the bed.

Sara Lee would repeat it some six times.

"*Taies d'oreiller*," when the pillows came. So Sara Lee called pillows by the name of their slips from that time forward! Came a bright hour when she rang the bell for the boy and asked for matches, which she certainly did not need, with entire success.

On the second night Sara Lee slept badly. At two o'clock she heard a sound in the hall, and putting on her kimono, opened the door. On a stiff chair outside, snoring profoundly, sat Jean, fully dressed.

The light from her candle roused him and he was wide awake in an instant.

"Why, Jean!" she said. "Isn't there any place for you to sleep?"

"I am to remain here, mademoiselle," he replied in English.

"But surely-not because of me?"

"It is the captain's order," he said briefly.

"I don't understand. Why?"

"All sorts of people come to this place, mademoiselle. But few ladies. It is best that I remain here."

She could not move him. He had remained standing while she spoke to him, and now he yawned, striving to conceal it. Sara Lee felt very uncomfortable, but Jean's attitude and voice alike were firm. She thanked him and said good night, but she slept little after that.

Lying there in the darkness, a warm glow of gratitude to Henri, and a feeling of her safety in his care, wrapped her like a mantle. She wondered drowsily if Harvey would ever have thought of all the small things that seemed second nature to this young Belgian officer.

She rather thought not.

IX

While she was breakfasting the next morning there was a tap at the door, and thinking it the maid she called to her to come in.

But it was Jean, an anxious Jean, twisting his cap in his hands.

"You have had a message from the captain, mademoiselle?"

"No, Jean."

"He was to have returned during the night. He has not come, mademoiselle."

Sara Lee forgot her morning negligée in Jean's harassed face.

"But-where did he go?"

Jean shrugged his shoulders and did not reply.

"Are you worried about him?"

"I am anxious, mademoiselle. But I am often anxious; and-he always returns."

He smiled almost sheepishly. Sara Lee, who had no subtlety but a great deal of intuition, felt that there was a certain relief in the smile, as though Jean, having had no message from his master, was pleased that she had none. Which was true enough, at that. Also she felt that Jean's one eye was inspecting her closely, which was also true. A new factor had come into Henri's life-by Jean's reasoning, a new and dangerous one. And there were dangers enough already.

Highly dangerous, Jean reflected in the back of his head as he backed out with a bow. A young girl unafraid of the morning sun and sitting at a little breakfast table as fresh as herself-that was a picture for a war-weary man.

Jean forgot for a moment his anxiety for Henri's safety in his fear for his peace of mind. For a doubt had been removed. The girl was straight. Jean's one sophisticated eye had grasped that at once. A good girl, alone, and far from home! And Henri, like all soldiers, woman-hungry for good women, for unpainted skins and clear eyes and the freshness and bloom of youth.

All there, behind that little breakfast table which might so pleasantly have been laid for two.

Jean took a walk that morning, and stood staring for twenty minutes into a clock maker's window, full of clocks. After which he drew out his watch and looked at the time!

At two in the afternoon Sara Lee saw Henri's car come into the square. It was, if possible, more dilapidated than before, and he came like a gray whirlwind, scattering people and dogs out of his way. Almost before he had had time to enter the hotel Sara Lee heard him in the hall, and the next moment he was bowing before her.

"I have been longer than I expected," he explained. "Have you been quite comfortable?"

Sara Lee, however, was gazing at him with startled eyes. He was dirty, unshaven, and his eyes looked hollow and bloodshot. From his neck to his heels he was smeared with mud, and his tidy tunic was torn into ragged holes.

"But you-you have been fighting!" she gasped.

"I? No, mademoiselle. There has been no battle." His eyes left her and traveled over the room. "They are doing everything for you? They are attentive?"

"Everything is splendid," said Sara Lee. "If you won't tell me how you got into that condition, at least you can send your coat down to me to mend."

"My tunic!" He looked at it smilingly. "You would do that?"

"I am nearly frantic for something to do."

He smiled, and suddenly bending down he took her hand and kissed it.

"You are not only very beautiful, mademoiselle, but you are very good."

He went away then, and Sara Lee got out her sewing things. The tunic came soon, carefully brushed and very ragged. But it was not Jean who brought it; it was the Flemish boy.

And upstairs in a small room with two beds Sara Lee might have been surprised to find Jean, the chauffeur, lying on one, while Henri shaved himself beside the other. For Jean, of the ragged uniform and the patch over one eye, was a count of Belgium, and served Henri because he loved him. And because, too, he was no longer useful in that little army where lay his heart.

Sometime a book will be written about the Jeans of this war, the great friendships it has brought forth between men. And not the least of its stories will be that of this Jean of the one eye. But its place is not here.

And perhaps there will be a book about the Henris, also. But not for a long time, and even then with care. For the heroes of one department of an army in the field live and die unsung.

Their bravest exploits are buried in secrecy. And that is as it must be. But it is a fine tale to go untold.

After he had bathed and shaved, Henri sat down at a tiny table and wrote. He drew a plan also, from a rough one before him. Then he took a match and burned the original drawing until it was but charred black ashes. When he had finished Jean got up from the bed and put on his overcoat.

"To the King?" he said.

"To the King, old friend."

Jean took the letter and went out.

Down below, Sara Lee sat with Henri's ragged tunic on her lap and stitched carefully. Sometime, she reflected, she would be mending worn garments for another man, now far away. A little flood of tenderness came over her. So helpless these men! There was so much to do for them! And soon, please God, she would be helping other tired and weary men, with food, and perhaps a word-when she had acquired some French-and perhaps a thread and needle.

She dined alone that night, as usual. Henri did not appear, though she had sent what she suspected was his only tunic back to him neatly mended at five o'clock. As a matter of fact Henri was sound asleep. He had meant to rest only for an hour a body that was crying aloud with fatigue. But Jean, coming in quietly, had found him sleeping like a child, and had put his own blanket over him and left him. Henri slept until morning, when Jean, coming up from his vigil outside the American girl's door, found him waking and rested, and rang for coffee.

Jean sat down on the edge of his bed and put on his shoes and puttees. He was a taciturn man, but now he had something to say that he did not like to say. And Henri knew it.

"What is it?" he asked, his arms under his head. "Come, let us have it! It is, of course, about the American lady."

"It is," Jean said bluntly. "You cannot mix women and war."

"And you think I am doing that?"

"I am not an idiot," Jean growled. "You do not know what you are doing. I do. She is young and lonely. You are young and not unattractive to women. Already she turns pale when I so much as ask if she has heard from you."

"You asked her that?"

"You were gone much longer than —"

"And you thought I might send her word, and not you!" Henri's voice was offended. He lay back while the boy brought in the morning coffee and rolls.

"Let me tell you something," he said when the boy had gone. "She is betrothed to an American. She wears a betrothal ring. I am to her-the French language!"

But, though Henri laughed, Jean remained grave and brooding. For Henri had not said what Sara Lee already was to him.

It was later in the morning that Henri broached the subject again. They were in the courtyard of an old house, working over the engine of the car.

"I think I have found a location for the young American lady," he said.

Jean hammered for a considerable time at a refractory rim.

"And where?" he asked at last.

Henri named the little town. Like Henri's family name, it must not be told. Too many things happened there, and perhaps it is even now Henri's headquarters. For that portion of the line has changed very little.

Jean fell to renewed hammering.

"If you will be silent I shall explain a plan," Henri said in a cautious tone. "She will make soup, with help which we shall find. And if coming in for refreshments a soldier shall leave a letter for me it is natural, is it not?"

"She will suspect, of course."

"I think not. And she reads no French. None whatever."

Yet Jean's suspicions were not entirely allayed. The plan had its advantages. It was important that Henri receive certain reports, and already the hotel whispered that Henri was of the secret service. It brought him added deference, of course, but additional danger.

So Jean accepted the plan, but with reservation. And it was not long afterward that he said to Sara Lee, in French: "There is a spider on your neck, mademoiselle."

But Sara Lee only said, "I'm sorry, Jean; you'll have to speak English to me for a while, I'm afraid."

And though he watched her for five minutes she did not put her hand to her neck.

However, that was later on. That afternoon Henri spent an hour with the Minister of War. And at the end of that time he said: "Thank you, Baron. I think you will not regret it. America must learn the truth, and how better than through those friendly people who come to us to help?"

It is as well to state, however, that he left the Minister of War with the undoubted impression that Miss Sara Lee Kennedy was a spinster of uncertain years.

Sara Lee packed her own suitcase that afternoon, doing it rather nervously because Henri was standing in the room by the window waiting for it. He had come in as matter-of-factly as Harvey had entered the parlor at Aunt Harriet's, except that he carried in his arms some six towels, a cake of soap and what looked suspiciously like two sheets.

"The house I have under consideration," he said, "has little to recommend it but the building, and even that-The occupants have gone away, and-you are not a soldier."

Sara Lee eyed the bundle.

"I don't need sheets," she expostulated.

"There are but two. And Jean has placed blankets in the car. You must have a pillow also."

He calmly took one of the hotel pillows from the bed.

"What else?" he asked calmly. "Cigarettes? But no, you do not smoke."

Sara Lee eyed him with something very like despair.

"Aren't you ever going to let me think for myself?"

"Would you have thought of these?" he demanded triumphantly. "You-you think only of soup and tired soldiers. Some one must think of you."

And there was a touch of tenderness in his voice. Sara Lee felt it and trembled slightly. He was so fine, and he must not think of her that way. It was not real. It couldn't be. Men were lonely here, where everything was hard and cruel. They wanted some of the softness of life, and all of kindness and sweetness that she could give should be Henri's. But she must make it clear that there could never be anything more.

There was a tightness about her mouth as she folded the white frock.

"I know that garment," he said boyishly. "Do you remember the night you wore it? And how we wandered in the square and made the plan that has brought us together again?"

Sara Lee reached down into her suitcase and brought up Harvey's picture.

"I would like you to see this," she said a little breathlessly. "It is the man I am to marry."

For a moment she thought Henri was not going to take it. But he came, rather slowly, and held out his hand for it. He went with it to the window and stood there for some time looking down at it.

"When are you going to marry him, mademoiselle?"

"As soon as I go back."

Sara Lee had expected some other comment, but he made none. He put the photograph very quietly on the bed before her, and gathered up the linen and the pillow in his arms.

"I shall send for your luggage, mademoiselle. And you will find me at the car outside, waiting."

And so it was that a very silent Henri sat with Jean going out to that strange land which was to be Sara Lee's home for many months. And a very silent Sara Lee, flanked with pillow and blankets, who sat back alone and tried to recall the tones of Harvey's voice.

44

And failed.

X

From Dunkirk to the Front, the road, after the Belgian line was passed, was lightly guarded. Henri came out of a reverie to explain to Sara Lee.

"We have not many men," he said. "And those that remain are holding the line. It is very weary, our army."

Now at home Uncle James had thought very highly of the Belgian Army. He had watched the fight they made, and he had tried to interest Sara Lee in it. But without much result. She had generally said: "Isn't it wonderful!" or "horrible," as the case might be, and put out of her mind as soon as possible the ringing words he had been reading. But she had not forgotten, she found. They came back to her as she rode through that deserted countryside. Henri, glancing back somewhat later, found her in tears.

He climbed back at once into the rear of the car and sat down beside her.

"You are homesick, I think?"

"Yes. But not for myself. I am just homesick for all the people who have lost their homes. You-and Jean, and all the rest."

"Some day I shall tell you about my home and what has happened to it," he said gravely. "Not now. It is not pleasant. But you must remember this: We are going back home, we Belgians." And after a little pause: "Just as you are."

He lapsed into silence after that, and Sara Lee, stealing a glance at him, saw his face set and hard. She had a purely maternal impulse to reach over and pat his hand.

Jean did not like Henri's shift to the rear of the car. He drove with a sort of irritable fever-ishness, until Henri leaned over and touched him on the shoulder.

"We have mademoiselle with us, Jean," he said in French.

"It is not difficult to believe," growled Jean. But he slackened his pace somewhat.

So far the road had been deserted. Now they had come up to a stream of traffic flowing slowly toward the Front. Armored cars, looking tall and top-heavy, rumbled and jolted along. Many lorries, one limousine containing a general, a few Paris buses, all smeared a dingy gray and filled with French soldiers, numberless and nondescript open machines, here and there a horse-drawn vehicle-these filled the road. In and out among them Jean threaded his way, while Sara Lee grew crimson with the effort to see it all, and Henri sat very stiff and silent.

At a crossroads they were halted by troops who had fallen out for a rest. The men stood at ease, and stared their fill at Sara Lee. Save for a few weary peasants, most of them had seen no women for months. But they were respectful, if openly admiring. And their admiration of her was nothing to Sara Lee's feeling toward them. She loved them all-boys with their first straggly beards on their chins; older men, looking worn and tired; French and Belgian; smiling and sad. But most of all, for Uncle James' sake, she loved the Belgians.

"I cannot tell you," she said breathlessly to Henri. "It is like a dream come true. And I shall help. You look doubtful sometimes, but I am sure."

"You are heaven sent," Henri replied gravely.

They turned into a crossroad after a time, and there in a little village Sara Lee found her new home. A strange village indeed, unoccupied and largely destroyed. Piles of bricks and plaster lined the streets. Broken glass was everywhere. Jean blew out a tire finally, because of the glass, and they were obliged to walk the remainder of the way.

"A poor place, mademoiselle," Henri said as they went along. "A peaceful little town, and quite beautiful, once. And it harbored no troops. But everything is meat for the mouths of their guns."

Sara Lee stopped and looked about her. Her heart was beating fast, but her lips were steady enough.

"And it is here that I —"

"A little distance down the street. You must see before you decide."

Steady, passionless firing was going on, not near, but far away, like low thunder before a summer storm. She was for months to live, to eat and sleep and dream to that rumbling from the Ypres salient, to waken when it ceased or to look up from her work at the strange silence. But it was new to her then, and terrible.

"Do they still shell this-this town?" she asked, rather breathlessly.

"Not now. They have done their work. Of course —" he did not finish.

Sara Lee's heart slowed down somewhat. After all, she had asked to be near the Front. And that meant guns and such destruction as was all about her. Only one thing troubled her.

"It is rather far from the trenches, isn't it?"

He smiled slightly.

"Far! It is not very far. Not so far as I would wish, mademoiselle. But, to do what you desire, it is the best I have to offer."

"How far away are the trenches?"

"A quarter of a mile beyond those poplar trees." He indicated on a slight rise a row of great trees broken somewhat but not yet reduced to the twisted skeletons they were to become later on. In a long line they faced the enemy like sentinels, winter-quiet but dauntless, and behind them lay the wreck of the little village, quiet and empty.

"Will the men know I am here?" Sara Lee asked anxiously.

"But, yes, mademoiselle. At night they come up from the trenches, and fresh troops take their places. They come up this street and go on to wherever they are to rest. And when they find that a house of-mercy is here-and soup, they will come. More than you wish."

"Belgian soldiers?"

"Only Belgian soldiers. That is as you want it to be, I think."

"If only I spoke French!"

"You will learn. And in the meantime, mademoiselle, I have taken the liberty of finding you a servant —a young peasant woman. And you will also have a soldier always on guard."

Something that had been in the back of Sara Lee's mind for some time suddenly went away. She had been thinking of Aunt Harriet and the Ladies' Aid Society of the Methodist Church. She had, in fact, been wondering how they would feel when they learned that she was living alone, the only woman among thousands of men. It had, oddly enough, never occurred to her before.

"You have thought of everything," she said gratefully.

But Henri said nothing. He had indeed thought of everything with a vengeance, with the net result that he was not looking at Sara Lee more than he could help.

These Americans were strange. An American girl would cross the seas, and come here alone with him —a man and human. And she would take for granted that he would do what he was doing for love of his kind-which was partly true; and she would be beautiful and sweet and amiable and quite unself-conscious. And then she would go back home, warm of heart with gratitude, and marry the man of the picture.

The village had but one street, and that deserted and in ruins. Behind its double row of houses, away from the enemy, lay the fields, a muddy canal and more poplar trees. And from far away, toward Ypres, there came constantly that somewhat casual booming of artillery which marked the first winter of the war.

The sound of the guns had first alarmed, then interested Sara Lee. It was detached then, far away. It meant little to her. It was only later, when she saw some of the results of the sounds she heard, that they became significant. But this is not a tale of the wounding of men. There are many such. This is the story of a little house of mercy, and of a girl with a dauntless spirit, and of two men who loved her. Only that.

The maid Henri had found was already in the house, sweeping. Henri presented her to Sara Lee, and he also brought a smiling little Belgian boy, in uniform and with a rifle.

46

"Your staff, mademoiselle!" he said. "And your residence!"

Sara Lee looked about her. With the trifling exception that there was no roof, it was whole. And the roof was not necessary, for the floors of the upper story served instead. There was a narrow passage with a room on either side, and a tiny kitchen behind.

Henri threw open a door on the right.

"Your bedroom," he said. "Well furnished, as you will see. It should be, since there has been brought here all the furniture not destroyed in the village."

His blacker mood had fallen away before her naive delight. He went about smiling boyishly, showing her the kettles in the kitchen; the supply, already so rare, of firewood; the little stove. But he stiffened somewhat when she placed her hand rather timidly on his arm.

"How am I ever to thank you?" she asked.

"By doing much good. And by never going beyond the poplar trees."

She promised both very earnestly.

But she was a little sad as she followed Henri about, he volubly expatiating on such advantages as plenty of air owing to the absence of a roof; and the attraction of the stove, which he showed much like a salesman anxious to make a sale. "Such a stove!" he finished contentedly. "It will make soup even in your absence, mademoiselle! Our peasants eat much soup; therefore it is what you would call a trained stove."

Before Sara Lee's eyes came a picture of Harvey and the Leete house, its white dining room, its bay window for plants, its comfortable charm and prettiness. And Harvey's face, as he planned it for her anxious, pleading, loving. She drew a long breath. If Henri noticed her abstraction he ignored it. He was all over the little house. One moment he was instructing Marie volubly, to her evident confusion. On René, the guard, he descended like a young cyclone, with warnings for mademoiselle's safety and comfort. He was everywhere, sitting on the bed to see if it was soft, tramping hard on the upper floor to discover if any plaster might loosen below, and pausing in that process to look keenly at a windmill in the field behind.

When he came down it was to say: "You are not entirely alone in the village, after all, mademoiselle. The miller has come back. I shall visit him now and explain."

He found Sara Lee, however, still depressed. She was sitting in a low chair in the kitchen gazing thoughtfully at the stove.

"I am here," she said. "And here is the house, and a stove, and-everything. But there are no shops; and what shall I make my soup out of?"

Henri stared at her rather blankly.

"True!" he said. "Very true. And I never thought of it!"

Then suddenly they both laughed, the joyous ringing laugh of ridiculous youth, which can see its own absurdities and laugh at them.

Henri counted off on his fingers.

"I thought of water," he said, "and a house, and firewood, and kettles and furniture. And there I ceased thinking."

It was dusk now. Marie lifted the lid from the stove, and a warm red glow of reflected light filled the little kitchen. It was warm and cozy; the kettle sang like the purring of a cat. And something else that had troubled Sara Lee came out.

"I wonder," she said, "if you are doing all this only because I —well, because I persuaded you." Which she had not. "Do the men really need me here?"

"Need you, mademoiselle?"

"Do they need what little I can give? They were smiling, all the ones I saw."

"A Belgian soldier always smiles. Even when he is fighting." His voice had lost its gayety and had taken on a deeper note. "Mademoiselle, I have brought you here, where I can think of no other woman who would have the courage to come, because you are needed. I cannot promise you entire safety" —his mouth tightened —"but I can promise you work and gratitude. Such gratitude, mademoiselle, as you may never know again."

That reassured her. But in her practical mind the matter of supplies loomed large. She brought the matter up again directly.

"It is to be hot chocolate and soup?" he asked.

"Both, if I find I have enough money. Soup only, perhaps."

"And soup takes meat, of course."

"It should, to be strengthening."

Henri looked up, to see Jean in the doorway smiling grimly.

"It is very simple," Jean said to him in French. "You have no other duties of course; so each day you shall buy in the market place at Dunkirk, with American money. And I shall become a delivery boy and bring out food for mademoiselle, and whatever is needed."

Henri smiled back at him cheerfully. "An excellent plan, Jean," he said. "Not every day, but frequently."

Jean growled and disappeared.

However, there was the immediate present to think of, and while Jean thawed his hands at the fire and Sara Lee was taking housewifely stock of her new home, Henri disappeared.

He came back in a half hour, carrying in a small basket butter, eggs, bread and potatoes.

"The miller!" he explained cheerfully to Sara Lee. "He has still a few hens, and hidden somewhere a cow. We can have milk-is there a pail for Marie to take to the mill? —and bread and an omelet. That is a meal!"

There was but one lamp, which hung over the kitchen stove. The room across from Sara Lee's bedroom contained a small round dining table and chairs. Sara Lee, enveloped in a large pinafore apron, made the omelet in the kitchen. Marie brought a pail of fresh milk. Henri, with a towel over his left arm, and in absurd mimicry of a Parisian waiter, laid the table; and Jean, dour Jean, caught a bit of the infection, and finding four bottles set to work with his pocketknife to fit candles into their necks.

Standing in corners, smiling, useless against the cheerful English that flowed from the kitchen stove to the dining room and back again, were René and Marie. It was of no use to attempt to help. Did the fire burn low, it was the young officer who went out for fresh wood. But René could not permit that twice. He brought in great armfuls of firewood and piled them neatly by the stove.

Henri was absurdly happy again. He would come to the door gravely, with Sara Lee's little phrase book in hand, and read from it in a solemn tone:

"'Shall we have duck or chicken?' 'Where can we get a good dinner at a moderate price?' 'Waiter, you have spilled wine on my dress.' 'Will you have a cigar?' 'No, thank you. I prefer a pipe.'"

And Sara Lee beat up the eggs and found, after a bad moment, some salt in a box, and then poured her omelet into the pan. She was very anxious that it be a good omelet. She must make good her claim as a cook or Henri's sublime faith in her would die.

It was a divine omelet. Even Jean said so. They sat, the three of them, in the cold little dining room and never knew that it was cold, and they ate prodigious quantities of omelet and bread and butter, and bully beef out of a tin, and drank a great deal of milk.

Even Jean thawed at last, under the influence of food and Sara Lee. Before the meal was over he was planning how to get her supplies to her and making notes on a piece of paper as to what she would need at once. They adjourned to Sara Lee's bedroom, where Marie had kindled a fire in the little iron stove, and sat there in the warmth with two candles, still planning. By that time Sara Lee had quite forgotten that at home one did not have visitors in one's bedroom.

Suddenly Henri held up his hand.

"Listen!" he said.

That was the first time Sara Lee had ever heard the quiet shuffling step of tired men, leaving their trenches under cover of darkness. Henri threw his military cape over her shoulders and she stood in the dark doorway, watching.

The empty street was no longer empty. From gutter to gutter flowed a stream of men, like a sluggish river which narrowed where a fallen house partly filled the way; not talking, not singing, just moving, bent under their heavy and mud-covered equipment. Here and there the clack of wooden sabots on the cobbles told of one poor fellow not outfitted with leather shoes. The light of a match here and there showed some few lucky enough to have still remaining cigarettes, and revealed also, in the immediate vicinity, a white bandage or two. Some few, recognizing Henri's officer's cap, saluted. Most of them stumbled on, too weary to so much as glance aside.

Nothing that Sara Lee had dreamed of war was like this. This was dreary and sodden and hopeless. Those fresh troops at the crossroads that day had been blithe and smiling. There had been none of the glitter and panoply of war, but there had been movement, the beating of a drum, the sharp cries of officers as the lines re-formed.

Here there were no lines. Just such a stream of men as at home might issue at night from a coal mine, too weary for speech. Only here they were packed together closely, and they did not speak, and some of them were wounded.

"There are so many!" she whispered to Henri. "A hundred such efforts as mine would not be enough."

"I would to God there were more!" Henri replied, through shut teeth.

"Listen, mademoiselle," he said later. "You cannot do all the kind work of the world. But you can do your part. And you will start by caring for only such as are wounded or ill. The others can go on. But every night some twenty or thirty, or even more, will come to your door-men slightly wounded or too weary to go on without a rest. And for those there will be a chair by the fire, and something hot, or perhaps a clean bandage. It sounds small? But in a month, think! You will have given comfort to perhaps a thousand men. You-alone!"

"I —alone!" she said in a queer choking voice. "And what about you? It is you who have made it possible."

But Henri was looking down the street to where the row of poplars hid what lay beyond. Far beyond a star shell had risen above the flat fields and floated there, a pure and lovely thing, shedding its white light over the terrain below. It gleamed for some thirty seconds and went out.

"Like that!" Henri said to her, but in French. "Like that you are to me. Bright and shining-and so soon gone."

Sara Lee thought he had asked her if she was cold.

XI

The girl was singularly adaptable. In a few days it was as though she had been for years in her little ruined house. She was very happy, though there was scarcely a day when her heart was not wrung. Such young-old faces! Such weary men! And such tales of wretchedness!

She got the tales by intuition rather than by words, though she was picking up some French at that. Marie would weep openly, at times. The most frequent story was of no news from the country held by the Germans, of families left with nothing and probably starving. The first inquiry was always for news. Had the American lady any way to make inquiry?

In time Sara Lee began to take notes of names and addresses, and through Mr. Travers, in London, and the Relief Commission, in Belgium, bits of information came back. A certain family was in England at a village in Surrey. Of another a child had died. Here was one that could not be located, and another reported massacred during the invasion.

Later on Sara Lee was to find her little house growing famous, besieged by anxious soldiers who besought her efforts, so that she used enormous numbers of stamps and a great deal of effort. But that was later on. And when that time came she turned to the work as a refuge from her thoughts. For days were coming when Sara Lee did not want to think.

But like all big things the little house made a humble beginning. A mere handful of men, daring the gibes of their comrades, stopped in that first night the door stood open, with its invitation of firelight and candles. But these few went away with a strange story-of a beautiful American, and hot soup, and even a cigarette apiece. That had been Henri's contribution, the cigarettes. And soon the fame of the little house went up and down the trenches, and it was like to die of overpopularity.

It was at night that the little house of mercy bloomed like a flower. During the daytime it was quiet, and it was then, as time went on, that Sara Lee wrote her letters home and to England, and sent her lists of names to be investigated. But from the beginning there was much to do. Vegetables were to be prepared for the soup, Marie must find and bring in milk for the chocolate, René must lay aside his rifle and chop firewood.

One worry, however, disappeared with the days. Henri was proving a clever buyer. The money she sent in secured marvels. Only Jean knew, or ever knew, just how much of Henri's steadily decreasing funds went to that buying. Certainly not Sara Lee. And Jean expostulated only once-to be met by such blazing fury as set him sullen for two days.

"I am doing this," Henri finished, a trifle ashamed of himself, "not for mademoiselle, but for our army. And since when have you felt that the best we can give is too much for such a purpose?"

Which was, however lofty, only a part of the truth.

So supplies came in plentifully, and Sara Lee pared vegetables and sang a bit under her breath, and glowed with good will when at night the weary vanguard of a weary little army stopped at her door and scraped the mud off its boots and edged in shyly.

She was very happy, and her soup was growing famous. It is true that the beef she used was not often beef, but she did not know that, and merely complained that the meat was stringy. Now and then there was no beef at all, and she used hares instead. On quiet days, when there was little firing beyond the poplar trees, she went about with a basket through the neglected winter gardens of the town. There were Brussels sprouts, and sometimes she found in a cellar carrots or cabbages. She had potatoes always.

It was at night then, from seven in the evening until one, that the little house was busiest. Word had gone out through the trenches beyond the poplar trees that slightly wounded men needing rest before walking back to their billets, exhausted and sick men, were welcome to the little house. It was soon necessary to give the officers tickets for the men. René took them in at the door, with his rifle in the hollow of his arm, and he was as implacable as a ticket taker at the opera.

Never once in all the months of her life there did Sara Lee have an ugly word, an offensive glance. But, though she never knew this, many half articulate and wholly earnest prayers were offered for her in those little churches behind the lines where sometimes the men slept, and often they prayed.

She was very businesslike. She sent home to the Ladies' Aid Society a weekly record of what had been done: So many bowls of soup; so many cups of chocolate; so many minor injuries dressed. Because, very soon, she found first aid added to her activities. She sickened somewhat at first. Later she allowed to Marie much of the serving of food, and in the little *salle à manger* she had ready on the table basins, water, cotton, iodine and bandages.

Henri explained the method to her.

"It is a matter of cleanliness," he said. "First one washes the wound and then there is the iodine. Then cotton, a bandage, and —a surgeon could do little more."

Henri and Jean came often. And more than once during the first ten days Jean spent the night rolled in a blanket by the kitchen fire, and Henri disappeared. He was always back in the morning, however, looking dirty and very tired. Sara Lee sewed more than one rent for him, those days, but she was strangely incurious. It was as though, where everything was strange, Henri's erratic comings and goings were but a part with the rest.

Then one night the unexpected happened. The village was shelled.

Sara Lee had received her first letter from Harvey that day. The maid at Morley's had forwarded it to her, and Henri had brought it up.

"I think I have brought you something you wish for very much," he said, looking down at her.

"Mutton?" she inquired anxiously.

"Better than that."

"Sugar?"

"A letter, mademoiselle."

Afterward he could not quite understand the way she had suddenly drawn in her breath. He had no memory, as she had, of Harvey's obstinate anger at her going, his conviction that she was doing a thing criminally wrong and cruel.

"Give it to me, please."

She took it into her room and closed the door. When she came out again she was composed and quiet, but rather white. Poor Henri! He was half mad that day with jealousy. Her whiteness he construed as longing.

This is a part of Harvey's letter:

> You may think that I have become reconciled, but I have not. If I could see any reason for it I might. But what reason is there? So many others, older and more experienced, could do what you are doing, and more safely.

> In your letter from the steamer you tell me not to worry. Good God, Sara Lee, how can I help worrying? I do not even know where you are! If you are in England, well and good. If you are abroad I do not want to know it. I know these foreigners. I run into them every day. And they do not understand American women. I get crazy when I think about it. I have had to let the Leete house go. There is not likely to be such a chance soon again. Business is good, but I don't seem to care much about it any more. Honestly, dear, I think you have treated me very badly. I always feel as though the people I meet are wondering if we have quarreled or what on earth took you away on this wild-goose chase. I don't know myself, so how can I tell them?

> I shall always love you, Sara Lee. I guess I'm that sort. But sometimes I wonder if, when we are married, you will leave me again in some such uncalled-for way. I warn you now, dear, that I won't stand for it. I'm suffering too much.

> HARVEY.

Sara Lee wore the letter next her heart, but it did not warm her. She went through the next few hours in a sort of frozen composure and ate nothing at all.

Then came the bombardment.

Henri and Jean, driving out from Dunkirk, had passed on the road ammunition trains, waiting in the road until dark before moving on to the Front. Henri had given Sara Lee her letter, had watched jealously for its effect on her, and then, his own face white and set, had gone on down the ruined street.

Here within the walls of a destroyed house he disappeared. The place was evidently familiar to him, for he moved without hesitation. Broken furniture still stood in the roofless rooms, and in front of a battered bureau Henri paused. Still whistling under his breath, he took off his uniform and donned a strange one, of greenish gray. In the pocket of the blouse he stuffed a soft round cap of the same color. Then, resuming his cape and Belgian cap, with its tassel over his forehead, he went out into the street again. He carried in his belt a pistol, but it was not the one he had brought in with him. As a matter of fact, by the addition of the cap in his pocket, Henri was at that moment in the full uniform of a *lieutenant* of a Bavarian infantry regiment, pistol and all.

He went down the street and along the road toward the poplars. He met the first detachment of men out of the trenches just beyond the trees, and stepped aside into the mud to let them pass, calling a greeting to them out of the darkness.

"*Bonsoir!*" they replied, and saluted stiffly. There were few among them who did not know his voice, and fewer still who did not suspect his business.

"A brave man," they said among themselves as they went on.

"How long will he last?" asked one young soldier, a boy in his teens.

"One cannot live long who does as he does," replied a gaunt and bearded man. "But it is a fine life while it continues. A fine life!"

The boy stepped out of the shuffling line and looked behind him. He could see only the glow of Henri's eternal cigarette. "I should like to go with him," he muttered wistfully.

The ammunition train was in the village now. It kept the center of the road, lest it should slide into the mud on either side and be mired. The men moved out of its way into the ditch, grumbling.

Henri went whistling softly down the road.

The first shell fell in the neglected square. The second struck the rear wagons of the ammunition train. Henri heard the terrific explosion that followed, and turning ran madly back into the village. More shells fell into the road. The men scattered like partridges, running for the fields, but the drivers of the ammunition wagons beat their horses and came lurching and shouting down the road.

There was cold terror in Henri's heart. He ran madly, throwing aside his cape as he went. More shells fell ahead in the street. Once in the darkness he fell flat over the body of a horse. There was a steady groaning from the ditch near by. But he got up and ran on, a strange figure with his flying hair and his German uniform.

He was all but stabbed by René when he entered the little house.

"Mademoiselle?" Henri gasped, holding René's bayonet away from his heaving chest.

"I am here," said Sara Lee's voice from the little *salle à manger*. "Let them carry in the wounded. I am getting ready hot water and bandages. There is not much space, for the corner of the room has been shot away."

She was as dead white in the candlelight, but very calm.

"You cannot stay here," Henri panted. "At any time —"

Another shell fell, followed by the rumble of falling walls.

"Some one must stay," said Sara Lee. "There must be wounded in the streets. Marie is in the cellar."

Henri pleaded passionately with her to go to the cellar, but she refused. He would have gathered her up in his arms and carried her there, but Jean came in, leading a wounded man, and Henri gave up in despair.

All that night they worked, a ghastly business. More than one man died that night in the little house, while a blond young man in a German uniform gave him a last mouthful of water or took down those pitifully vague addresses which were all the dying Belgians had to give.

"I have not heard-last at Aarschot, but now-God knows where."

No more shells fell. At dawn, with all done that could be done, Sara Lee fainted quietly in the hallway. Henri carried her in and placed her on her bed. A corner of the room was indeed gone. The mantel was shattered and the little stove. But on the floor lay Harvey's photograph uninjured. Henri lifted it and looked at it. Then he placed it on the table, and very reverently he kissed the palm of Sara Lee's quiet hand.

Daylight found the street pitiful indeed. Henri, whose costume René had been casting wondering glances at all night, sent a request for men from the trenches to clear away the bodies of the horses and bury them, and somewhat later over a single grave in the fields there was a simple ceremony of burial for the men who had fallen. Henri had changed again by that time, but he sternly forbade Sara Lee to attend.

"On pain," he said, "of no more supplies, mademoiselle. These things must be. They are war. But you can do nothing to help, and it will be very sad."

Ambulances took away the wounded at dawn, and the little house became quiet once more. With planks René repaired the damage to the corner, and triumphantly produced and set up another stove. He even put up a mantelshelf, and on it, smiling somewhat, he placed Harvey's picture.

Sara Lee saw it there, and a tiny seed of resentment took root and grew.

"If there had been no one here last night," she said to the photograph, "many more would have died. How can you say I am cruel to you? Isn't this worth the doing?"

But Harvey remained impassive, detached, his eyes on the photographer's white muslin screen. And the angle of his jaw was set and dogged.

XII

That morning there was a conference in the little house-Colonel Lilias, who had come in before for a mute but appreciative call on Sara Lee, and for a cup of chocolate; Captain Tournay, Jean and Henri. It was held round the little table in the *salle à manger*, after Marie had brought coffee and gone out.

"They had information undoubtedly," said the colonel. "The same thing happened at Pervyse when an ammunition train went through. They had the place, and what is more they had the time. Of course there are the airmen."

"It did not leave the main road until too late for observation from the air," Henri put in shortly.

"Yet any one who saw it waiting at the crossroads might have learned its destination. The drivers talk sometimes."

"But the word had to be carried across," said Captain Tournay. "That is the point. My men report flashes of lights from the fields. We have followed them up and found no houses, no anything. In this flat country a small light travels far."

"I shall try to learn to-night," Henri said. "It is, of course, possible that some one from over there —" He shrugged his shoulders.

"I think not." Colonel Lilias put a hand on Henri's shoulder affectionately. "They have not your finesse, boy. And I doubt if, in all their army, they have so brave a man."

Henri flushed.

"There is a courage under fire, with their fellows round-that is one thing. And a courage of attack-that is even more simple. But the bravest man is the one who works alone-the man to whom capture is death without honor."

The meeting broke up. Jean and Henri went away in the car, and though supplies came up regularly Sara Lee did not see the battered gray car for four days. At the end of that time Henri came alone. Jean, he said briefly, was laid up for a little while with a flesh wound in his shoulder. He would be well very soon. In the meantime here at last was mutton. It had come from England, and he, Henri, had found it lying forgotten and lonely and very sad and had brought it along.

After that Henri disappeared on foot. It was midafternoon and a sunny day. Sara Lee saw him walking briskly across the fields and watched him out of sight. She spoke some French now, and she had gathered from René, who had no scruples about listening at a door, that Henri was the bravest man in the Belgian Army.

Until now Sara Lee had given small thought to Henri's occupation. She knew nothing of war, and the fact that Henri, while wearing a uniform, was unattached, had not greatly impressed her. Had she known the constitution of a modern army she might have wondered over his freedom, his powerful car, his passes and maps. But his detachment had not seemed odd to her. Even his appearance during the bombardment in the uniform of a German *lieutenant* had meant nothing to her. She had never seen a German uniform.

That evening, however, when he returned she ventured a question. They dined together, the two of them, for the first time at the little house alone. Always before Jean had made the third. And it was a real meal, for Sara Lee had sacrificed a bit of mutton from her soup, and Henri had produced from his pocket a few small and withered oranges.

"A gift!" he said gayly, and piled them in a precarious heap in the center of the table. On the exact top he placed a walnut.

"Now speak gently and walk softly," he said. "It is a work of art and not to be lightly demolished."

He was alternately gay and silent during the meal, and more than once Sara Lee found his eyes on her, with something new and different in them.

"Just you and I together!" he said once. "It is very wonderful."

And again: "When you go back to him, shall you tell him of your good friend who has tried hard to serve you?"

"Of course I shall," said Sara Lee. "And he will write you, I know. He will be very grateful."

But it was she who was silent after that, because somehow it would be hard to make Harvey understand. And as for his being grateful—

"Mademoiselle," said Henri later on, "would you object if I make a suggestion? You wear a very valuable ring. I think it is entirely safe, but-who can tell? And also it is not entirely kind to remind men who are far from all they love that you —"

Sara Lee flushed and took off her ring.

"I am glad you told me," she said. And Henri did not explain that the Belgian soldiers would not recognize the ring as either a diamond or a symbol, but that to him it was close to torture.

It was when he insisted on carrying out the dishes, singing a little French song as he did so, that Sara Lee decided to speak what was in her mind. He was in high spirits then.

"Mademoiselle," he said, "shall I show you something that the eye of no man has seen before, and that, when we have seen it, shall never be seen again?"

On her interested consent he called in Marie and René, making a great ceremony of the matter, and sending Marie into hysterical giggling.

"Now see!" he said earnestly. "No eye before has ever seen or will again. Will you guess, mademoiselle? Or you, Marie? René?"

"A tear?" ventured Sara Lee.

"But-do I look like weeping?"

He did not, indeed. He stood, tall and young and smiling before them, and produced from his pocket the walnut.

"Perceive!" he said, breaking it open and showing the kernel. "Has human eye ever before seen it?" He thrust it into Marie's open mouth. "And it is gone! *Voilà tout!*"

It was that evening, while Sara Lee cut bandages and Henri rolled them, that she asked him what his work was. He looked rather surprised, and rolled for a moment without replying. Then: "I am a man of all work," he said. "What you call odd jobs."

"Then you don't do any fighting?"

"In the trenches-no. But now and then I have a little skirmish."

A sort of fear had been formulating itself in Sara Lee's mind. The trenches she could understand or was beginning to understand. But this alternately joyous and silent idler, this soldier of no regiment and no detail-was he playing a man's part in the war?

"Why don't you go into the trenches?" she asked with her usual directness. "You say there are too few men. Yet —I can understand Monsieur Jean, because he has only one eye. But you!"

"I do something," he said, avoiding her eyes. "It is not a great deal. It is the thing I can do best. That is all."

He went away some time after that, leaving the little house full and busy justifying its existence. The miller's son, who came daily to chat with Marie, was helping in the kitchen. By the warm stove, and only kept from standing over it by Marie's sharp orders, were as many men as could get near. Each held a bowl of hot soup, and-that being a good day —a piece of bread. Tall soldiers and little ones, all dirty, all weary, almost all smiling, they peered over each other's shoulders, to catch, if might be, a glimpse of Marie's face.

When they came too close she poked an elbow into some hulking fellow and sent him back. "Elbow-room, in the name of God," she would beg.

Over all the room hung the warm steam from the kettles, and a delicious odor, and peace.

Sara Lee had never heard of the word *morale*. She would have been astonished to have been told that she was helping the *morale* of an army. But she gave each night in that little house of mercy something that nothing else could give-warmth and welcome, but above all a touch of home.

That night Henri did not come back. She stood by her table bandaging, washing small wounds, talking her bits of French, until one o'clock. Then, the last dressing done, she went to the kitchen. Marie was there, with Maurice, the miller's son.

"Has the captain returned?" she asked.

"Not yet, mademoiselle."

"Leave a warm fire," Sara Lee said. "He will probably come in later."

Maurice went away, with a civil good night. Sara Lee stood in the doorway after he had gone, looking out. Farther along the line there was a bombardment going on. She knew now what a bombardment meant and her brows contracted. Somewhere there in the trenches men were enduring that, while Henri —

She said a little additional prayer that night, which was that she should have courage to say to him what she felt-that there were big things to do, and that it should not all be left to these smiling, ill-clad peasant soldiers.

At that moment Henri, in his gray-green uniform, was cutting wire before a German trench, one of a party of German soldiers, who could not know in the darkness that there had been a strange addition to their group. Cutting wire and learning many things which it was well that he should know.

Now and then, in perfect German, he whispered a question. Always he received a reply. And stowed it away in his tenacious memory for those it most concerned.

At daylight he was asleep by Sara Lee's kitchen fire. And at daylight Sara Lee was awakened by much firing, and putting on a dressing gown she went out to see what was happening. René was in the street looking toward the poplar trees.

"An attack," he said briefly.

"You mean-the Germans?"

"Yes, mademoiselle."

She went back into the little ruined house, heavy-hearted. She knew now what it meant, an attack. That night there would be ambulances in the street, and word would come up that certain men were gone-would never seek warmth and shelter in her kitchen or beg like children for a second bowl of soup.

On the kitchen floor by the dying fire Henri lay asleep.

XIII

Much has been said of the work of spies-said and written. Here is a woman in Paris sending forbidden messages on a marked coin. Men are tapped on the shoulder by a civil gentleman in a sack suit, and walk away with him, never to be seen again.

But of one sort of spy nothing has been written and but little is known. Yet by him are battles won or lost. On the intelligence he brings attacks are prepared for and counter-attacks launched. It is not always the airman, in these days of camouflage, who brings word of ammunition trains or of new batteries.

In the early days of the war the work of the secret service at the Front was of the gravest importance. There were fewer air machines, and observation from the air was a new science. Also trench systems were incomplete. Between them, known to a few, were breaks of solid land, guarded from behind. To one who knew, it was possible, though dangerous beyond words, to cross the inundated country that lay between the Belgian Front and the German lines, and even with good luck to go farther.

Henri, for instance, on that night before had left the advanced trench at the railway line, had crawled through the Belgian barbed wire, and had advanced, standing motionless as each star shell burst overhead, and then moving on quickly. The inundation was his greatest difficulty. Shallow in most places, it was full of hidden wire and crisscrossed with irrigation ditches. Once he stumbled into one, but he got out by swimming. Had he been laden with a rifle and equipment it might have been difficult.

He swore to himself as his feet touched ground again. For a star shell was hanging overhead, and his efforts had sent wide and ever increasingly widening circles over the placid surface of the lagoon. Let them lap to the German outposts and he was lost.

Henri's method was peculiar to himself. Where there was dry terrain he did as did the others, crouched and crept. But here in the salt marshes, where the sea had been called to Belgium's aid, he had evolved a system of moving, neck deep in water, stopping under the white night lights, advancing in the darkness. There was no shelter. The country was flat as a hearth.

He would crawl out at last in the darkness and lie flat, as the dead lie. And then, inch by inch, he would work his way forward, by routes that he knew. Sometimes he went entirely through the German lines, and reconnoitered on the roads behind. They were shallow lines then, for the inundation made the country almost untenable, and a charge in force from the Belgians across was unlikely.

Henri knew his country well, as well as he loved it. In a farmhouse behind the German lines he sometimes doffed his wet gray-green uniform and put on the clothing of a Belgian peasant. Trust Henri then for being a lout, a simple fellow who spoke only Flemish-but could hear in many tongues. Watch him standing at crossroads and marveling at big guns that rumble by.

At first Henri had wished, having learned of an attack, to be among those who repelled it. Then one day his King had sent for him to come to that little village which was now his capital city.

He had been sent in alone and had found the King at the table, writing. Henri bowed and waited. They were not unlike, these two men, only Henri was younger and lighter, and where the King's eyes were gray Henri's were blue. Such a queer setting for a king it was —a tawdry summer home, ill-heated and cheaply furnished. But by the presence of Belgium's man of all time it became royal.

So Henri bowed and waited, and soon the King got up and shook hands with him. As a matter of fact they knew each other rather well, but to explain more would be to tell that family name of Henri's which must never be known.

"Sit down," said the King gravely. And he got a box of cigars from the mantelpiece and offered it. "I sent for you because I want to talk to you. You are doing valuable work."

"I am glad you think it so, sire," said Henri rather unhappily, because he felt what was coming. "But I cannot do it all the time. There are intervals —"

An ordinary mortal may not interrupt a king, but a king may interrupt anything, except perhaps a German bombardment.

"Intervals, of course. If there were not you would be done in a month."

"But I am a soldier. My place is —"

"Your place is where you are most useful."

Henri was getting nothing out of the cigar. He flung it away and got up.

"I want to fight too," he said stubbornly. "We need every man, and I am-rather a good shot. I do this other because I can do it. I speak their infernal tongue. But it's dirty business at the best, sire." He remembered to put in the sire, but rather ungraciously. Indeed he shot it out like a bullet.

"Dirty business!" said the King thoughtfully. "I see what you mean. It is, of course. But-not so dirty as the things they have done, and are doing."

He sat still and let Henri stamp up and down, because, as has been said, he knew the boy. And he had never been one to insist on deference, which was why he got so much of it. But at last he got up and when Henri stood still, rather ashamed of himself, he put an arm over the boy's shoulders.

"I want you to do this thing, for me. And this thing only," he said. "It is the work you do best. There are others who can fight, but —I do not know any one else who can do as you have done."

Henri promised. He would have promised to go out and drown himself in the sea, just beyond the wind-swept little garden, for the tall grave man who stood before him. Then he bowed and went out, and the King went back to his plain pine table and his work. That was the reason why Sara Lee found him asleep on the floor by her kitchen stove that morning, and went back to her cold bed to lie awake and think. But no explanation came to her.

The arrival of Marie roused Henri. The worst of the bombardment was over, but there was far-away desultory firing. He listened carefully before, standing outside in the cold, he poured over his head and shoulders a pail of cold water. He was drying himself vigorously when he heard Sara Lee's voice in the kitchen.

The day began for Henri when first he saw the girl. It might be evening, but it was the beginning for him. So he went in when he had finished his toilet and bowed over her hand.

"You are cold, mademoiselle."

"I think I am nervous. There was an attack this morning."

"Yes?"

Marie had gone into the next room, and Sara Lee raised haggard eyes to his.

"Henri," she said desperately-it was the first time she had called him that —"I have some-thing to say to you, and it's not very pleasant."

"You are going home?" It was the worst thing he could think of. But she shook her head.

"You will think me most ungrateful and unkind."

"You? Kindness itself!"

"But this is different. It is not for myself. It is because I care a great deal about-about —"

"Mademoiselle!"

"About your honor. And somehow this morning, when I found you here asleep, and those poor fellows in the trenches fighting—"

Henri stared at her. So that was it! And he could never tell her. He was sworn to secrecy by every tradition and instinct of his work. He could never tell her, and she would go on thinking him a shirker and a coward. She would be grateful. She would be sweetness itself. But deep in her heart she would loathe him, as only women can hate for a failing they never forgive.

"But I have told you," he said rather wildly, "I am not idle. I do certain things-not much, but of a degree of importance."

"You do not fight."

In Sara Lee's defense many things may be urged-her ignorance of modern warfare; the iso-lation of her lack of knowledge of the language; but, perhaps more than anything, a certain rigidity of standard that comprehended no halfway ground. Right was right and wrong was wrong to her in those days. Men were brave or were cowards. Henri was worthy or unworthy. And she felt that, for all his kindness to her, he was unworthy.

He could have set himself right with a word, at that. But his pride was hurt. He said nothing except, when she asked if he had minded what she said, to reply:

"I am sorry you feel as you do. I am not angry."

He went away, however, without breakfast. Sara Lee heard his car going at its usual breakneck speed up the street, and went to the door. She would have called him back if she could, for his eyes haunted her. But he did not look back.

XIV

For four days the gray car did not come again. Supplies appeared in another gray car, driven by a surly Fleming. The waking hours were full, as usual. Sara Lee grew a little thin, and seemed to be always listening. But there was no Henri, and something that was vivid and joyous seemed to have gone out of the little house.

Even Marie no longer sang as she swept or washed the kettles, and Sara Lee, making up the records to send home, put little spirit into the letter that went with them.

On the second day she wrote to Harvey.

"I am sorry that you feel as you do," she wrote, perhaps unconsciously using Henri's last words to her. "I have not meant to be cruel. And if you were here you would realize that whether others could have done what I am doing or not-and of course many could-it is worth doing. I hear that other women are establishing houses like this, but the British and the French will not allow women so near the lines. The men come in at night from the trenches so tired, so hungry and so cold. Some of them are wounded too. I dress the little wounds. I do give them something, Harvey dear-if it is only a reminder that there are homes in the world, and everything is not mud and waiting and killing."

She told him that his picture was on her mantel, but she did not say that a corner of her room had been blown away or that the mantel was but a plank from a destroyed house. And she sent a great deal of love, but she did not say that she no longer wore his ring on her finger. And, of course, she was coming back to him if he still wanted her.

More than Henri's absence was troubling Sara Lee those days. Indeed she herself laid all her anxiety to one thing, a serious one at that. With all the marvels of Henri's buying, and Jean's, her money was not holding out. The scope of the little house had grown with its fame. Now and then there were unexpected calls, too-Marie's mother, starving in Havre; sickness and death in the little town at the crossroads: a dozen small emergencies, but adding to the demands on her slender income. She had, as a matter of fact, already begun to draw on her private capital.

And during the days when no gray car appeared she faced the situation, took stock, as it were, and grew heavy-eyed and wistful.

On the fifth day the gray car came again, but Jean drove it alone. He disclaimed any need for sympathy over his wound, and with René's aid carried in the supplies.

There was the business of checking them off, and the further business of Sara Lee's paying for them in gold. She sat at the table, Jean across, and struggled with centimes and francs and louis d'or, an engrossed frown between her eyebrows.

Jean, sitting across, thought her rather changed. She smiled very seldom, and her eyes were perhaps more steady. It was a young girl he and Henri had brought out to the little house. It was a very serious and rather anxious young woman who sat across from him and piled up the money he had brought back into little stacks.

"Jean," she said finally, "I am not going to be able to do it."

"To do what?"

"To continue-here."

"No?"

"You see I had a little money of my own, and twenty pounds I got in London. You and-and Henri have done miracles for me. But soon I shall have used all my own money, except enough to take me back. And now I shall have to start on my English notes. After that —"

"You are too good to the men. These cigarettes, now-you could do without them."

"But they are very cheap, and they mean so much, Jean."

She sat still, her hands before her on the table. From the kitchen came the bubbling of the eternal soup. Suddenly a tear rolled slowly down her cheek. She had a hatred of crying in public, but Jean apparently did not notice.

"The trouble, mademoiselle, is that you are trying to feed and comfort too many."

"Jean," she said suddenly, "where is Henri?"

"In England, I think."

The only clear thought in Sara Lee's mind was that Henri was not in France, and that he had gone without telling her. She had hurt him horribly. She knew that. He might never come back to the little house of mercy. There was, in Henri, for all his joyousness, an implacable strain. And she had attacked his honor. What possible right had she to do that?

The memory of all his thoughtful kindness came back, and it was a pale and distracted Sara Lee who looked across the table at Jean.

"Did he tell you anything?"

"Nothing, mademoiselle."

"He is very angry with me, Jean."

"But surely no, mademoiselle. With you? It is impossible."

But though they said nothing more, Jean considered the matter deeply. He understood now, for instance, a certain strangeness in Henri's manner before his departure. They had quarreled, these two. Perhaps it was as well, though Jean was by now a convert to Sara Lee. But he looked out, those days, on but half a world, did Jean. So he saw only the woman hunger in Henri, and nothing deeper. And in Sara Lee a woman, and nothing more.

And-being Jean he shrugged his shoulders.

They fell to discussing ways and means. The chocolate could be cut out, but not the cigarettes. Sara Lee, arguing vehemently for them and trying to forget other things, remembered suddenly how Uncle James had hated cigarettes, and that Harvey himself disapproved of them. Somehow Harvey seemed, those days, to present a constant figure of disapproval. He gave her no moral support.

At Jean's suggestion she added to her report of so many men fed with soup, so much tobacco, sort not specified, so many small wounds dressed —a request that if possible her allowance be increased. She did it nervously, but when the letter had gone she felt a great relief. She enclosed a snapshot of the little house.

Jean, as it happens, had lied about Henri. Not once, but several times. He had told Marie, for instance, that Henri was in England, and later on he told René. Then, having done his errand, he drove six miles back along the main road to Dunkirk and picked up Henri, who was sitting on the bank of a canal watching an ammunition train go by.

Jean backed into a lane and turned the car round. After that Henri got in and they went rapidly back toward the Front. It was a different Henri, however, who left the car a mile from the crossroads —a Henri in the uniform of a French private soldier, one of those odd and impracticable uniforms of France during the first year, baggy dark blue trousers, stiff cap, and the long-tailed coat, its skirts turned back and faced. Round his neck he wore a knitted scarf, which covered his chin, and, true to the instinct of the French peasant in a winter campaign, he wore innumerable undergarments, the red of a jersey showing through rents in his coat.

Gone were Henri's long clean lines, his small waist and broad shoulders, the swing of his walk. Instead, he walked with the bent-kneed swing of the French infantryman, that tireless but awkward marching step which renders the French Army so mobile.

He carried all the impedimenta of a man going into the trenches, an extra jar of water, a flat loaf of bread strapped to his haversack, and an intrenching tool jingling at his belt.

Even Jean smiled as he watched him moving along toward the crowded crossroads-smiled and then sighed. For Jean had lost everything in the war. His wife had died of a German bullet long months before, and with her had gone a child much prayed for and soon to come. But Henri had brought back to Jean something to live for-or to die for, as might happen.

Henri walked along gayly. He hailed other French soldiers. He joined a handful and stood talking to them. But he reached the crossroads before the ammunition train.

The crossroads was crowded, as usual-many soldiers, at rest, waiting for the word to fall in, a battery held up by the breaking of a wheel. A temporary forge had been set up, and soldiers in leather aprons were working over the fire. A handful of peasants watched, their dull eyes following every gesture. And one of them was a man Henri sought.

Henri sat down on the ground and lighted a cigarette. The ammunition train rolled in and halted, and the man Henri watched turned his attention to the train. He had been dull and quiet at the forge, but now he became smiling, a good fellow. He found a man he knew among the drivers and offered him a cigarette. He also produced and presented an entire box of matches. Matches were very dear, and hardly to be bought at any price.

Henri watched grimly and hummed a little song:

"*Trou la la, çà ne va guère;*
Trou la la, çà ne va pas."

Still humming under his breath, when the peasant left the crossroads he followed him. Not closely. The peasant cut across the fields. Henri followed the road and entered the fields at a different angle. He knew his way quite well, for he had done the same thing each day for four days. Only twice he had been a Belgian peasant, and once he was an officer, and once he had been a priest.

Four days he had done this thing, but to-day was different. To-day there would be something worth while, he fancied. And he made a mental note that Sara Lee must not be in the little house that night.

When he had got to a canal where the pollard willows were already sending out their tiny red buds, Henri sat down again. The village lay before him, desolate and ruined, a travesty of homes. And on a slight rise, but so concealed from him by the willows that only the great wings showed, stood the windmill.

It was the noon respite then, and beyond the line of poplars all was quiet. The enemy liked time for foods and the Belgians crippled by the loss of that earlier train, were husbanding their ammunition. Far away a gap in the poplar trees showed a German observation balloon, a tiny dot against the sky.

The man Henri watched went slowly, for he carried a bag of grain on his back. Henri no longed watched him, He watched the wind wheel. It had been broken, and one plane was now patched with what looked like a red cloth. There was a good wind, but clearly the miller was idle that day. The great wings were not turning.

Henri sat still and smoked. He thought of many things-of Sara Lee's eyes when in the center of the London traffic she had held the dying donkey; of her small and radiant figure at the Savoy; of the morning he had found her at Calais, in the Gare Maritime, quietly unconscious that she had done a courageous thing. And he thought, too, of the ring and the photograph she carried. But mostly he remembered the things she had said to him on their last meeting.

Perhaps there came to him his temptation too. It would be so easy that night, if things went well, to make a brave showing before her, to let her see that these odd jobs he did had their value and their risks. But he put that from him. The little house of mercy must be empty that night, for her sake. He shivered as he remembered the room where she slept, the corner that was shot away and left open to the street.

So he sat and watched. And at one o'clock the mill wheel began turning. It was easy to count the revolutions by the red wing. Nine times it turned, and stopped. After five minutes or so it turned again, thirty times. Henri smiled: an ugly smile.

"A good guess," he said to himself. "But it must be more than a guess."

His work for the afternoon was done. Still with the bent-kneed swing he struck back to the road, and avoiding the crossroads, went across more fields to a lane where Jean waited with the car. Henri took a plunge into the canal when he had removed his French uniform, and producing a towel from under a bush rubbed himself dry. His lean boyish body gleamed, arms and legs brown from much swimming under peaceful summer suns. On his chest he showed two scars, still pink. Shrapnel bites, he called them. But he had, it is to be feared, a certain young satisfaction in them.

He was in high good humor. The water was icy, and Jean had refused to join him.

"My passion for cleanliness," Henri said blithely, "is the result of my English school days. You would have been the better for an English education, Jean."

"A canal in March!" Jean grunted. "You will end badly."

Henri looked longingly at the water.

"Had I a dry towel," he said, "I would go in again."

Jean looked at him with his one eye.

"You would be prettier without those scars," he observed. But in his heart he prayed that there might be no others added to them, that nothing might mar or destroy that bright and youthful body.

"*Dépêchez-vous! Vous sommes pressés!*" he added.

But Henri was minded to play. He girded himself with the towel and struck an attitude.

"The Russian ballet, Jean!" he said, and capering madly sent Jean into deep grumbles of laughter by his burlesque.

"I must have exercise," Henri said at last when, breathless and with flying hair, he began to dress. "That, too, is my English schooling. If you, Jean —"

"To the devil with your English schooling!" Jean remonstrated.

Henri sobered quickly after that. The exhilaration of his cold plunge was over.

"The American lady?" he asked. "She is all right?"

"She is worried. There is not enough money."

Henri frowned.

"And I have nothing!"

This opened up an old wound with Jean.

"If you would be practical and take pay for what you are doing," he began.

Henri cut him short.

"Pay!" he said. "What is there to pay me with? And what is the use of reopening the matter? A man may be a spy for love of his country. God knows there is enough lying and deceit in the business. But to be a spy for money-never!"

There was a little silence. Then: "Now for mademoiselle," said Henri. "She must be out of the village to-night. And that, dear friend, must be your affair. She does not like me."

All the life had gone out of his voice.

XV

"But why should I go?" Sara Lee asked. "It is kind of you to ask me, Jean. But I am here to work, not to play."

Long ago Sara Lee had abandoned her idea of Jean as a paid chauffeur. She even surmised, from something Marie had said, that he had been a person of importance in the Belgium of before the war. So she was grateful, but inclined to be obstinate.

"You have been so much alone, mademoiselle —"

"Alone!"

"Cut off from your own kind. And now and then one finds, at the hotel in Dunkirk, some English nurses who are having a holiday. You would like to talk to them perhaps."

"Jean," she said unexpectedly, "why don't you tell me the truth? You want me to leave the village to-night. Why?"

"Because, mademoiselle, there will be a bombardment."

"The village itself?"

"We expect it," he answered dryly.

Sara Lee went a little pale.

"But then I shall be needed, as I was before."

"No troops will pass through the town to-night. They will take a road beyond the fields."

"How do you know these things?" she asked, wondering. "About the troops I can understand. But the bombardment."

"There are ways of finding out, mademoiselle," he replied in his noncommittal voice. "Now, will you go?"

"May I tell Marie and René?"

"No."

"Then I shall not go. How can you think that I would consider my own safety and leave them here?"

Jean had ascertained before speaking that Marie was not in the house. As for René, he sat on the single doorstep and whittled pegs on which to hang his rifle inside the door. And as he carved he sang words of his own to the tune of Tipperary.

Inside the little *salle à manger* Jean reassured Sara Lee. It was important-vital-that René and Marie should not know far in advance of the bombardment. They were loyal, certainly, but these were his orders. In abundance of time they would be warned to leave the village.

"Who is to warn them?"

"Henri has promised, mademoiselle. And what he promises is done."

"You said this morning that he was in England."

"He has returned."

Sara Lee's heart, which had been going along merely as a matter of duty all day, suddenly began to beat faster. Her color came up, and then faded again. He had returned, and he had not come to the little house. But then-what could Henri mean to her, his coming or his going? Was she to add to her other sins against Harvey the supreme one of being interested in Henri?

Not that she said all that, even to herself. There was a wave of gladness and then a surge of remorse. That is all. But it was a very sober Sara Lee who put on her black suit with the white collar that afternoon and ordered, by Jean's suggestion, the evening's preparations as though nothing was to happen.

She looked round her little room before she left it. It might not be there when she returned. So she placed Harvey's photograph under her mattress for safety, and rather uncomfortably she laid beside it the small ivory crucifix that Henri had found in a ruined house and brought to her. Harvey was not a Catholic. He did not believe in visualizing his religion. And she had a distinct impression that he considered such things as did so as bordering on idolatry.

Sometime after dusk that evening the ammunition train moved out. At a point a mile or so from the village a dispatch rider on a motor cycle stopped the rumbling lorry at the head of the procession and delivered a message, which the guide read by the light of a sheltered match. The train moved on, but it did not turn down to the village. It went beyond to a place of safety, and there remained for the night.

But before that time Henri, lying close in a field, had seen a skulking figure run from the road to the mill, and soon after had seen the mill wheel turn once, describing a great arc; and on one of the wings, showing only toward the poplar trees, was a lighted lantern.

Five minutes later, exactly time enough for the train to have reached the village street, German shells began to fall in it. Henri, lying flat on the ground, swore silently and deeply.

In every land during this war there have been those who would sell their country for a price. Sometimes money. Sometimes protection. And of all betrayals that of the man who sells his own country is the most dastardly. Henri, lying face down, bit the grass beneath him in sheer rage.

One thing he had not counted on, he who foresaw most things. The miller and his son, being what they were, were cowards as well. Doubtless the mill had been promised protection. It was too valuable to the Germans to be destroyed. But with the first shot both men left the house by the mill and scurried like rabbits for the open fields.

Maurice, poor Marie's lover by now, almost trampled on Henri's prostrate body. And Henri was alone, and his work was to take them alive. They had information he must have-how the *modus vivendi* had been arranged, through what channels. And under suitable treatment they would tell.

He could not follow them through the fields. He lay still, during a fiercer bombardment than the one before, raising his head now and then to see if the little house of mercy still stood. No shells came his way, but the sky line of the village altered quickly. The standing fragment of the church towers went early. There was much sound of falling masonry. From somewhere behind him a Belgian battery gave tongue, but not for long. And then came silence.

Henri moved then. He crept nearer the mill and nearer. And at last he stood inside and took his bearings. A lamp burned in the kitchen, showing a dirty brick floor and a littered table-such a house as men keep, untidy and unhomelike. A burnt kettle stood on the hearth, and leaning against the wall was the bag of grain Maurice had carried from the crossroads.

"A mill which grinds without grain," Henri said to himself.

There was a boxed-in staircase to the upper floor, and there, with the door slightly ajar, he stationed himself, pistol in hand. Now and then he glanced uneasily at the clock. Sara Lee must not be back before he had taken his prisoners to the little house and turned them over to those who waited there.

There were footsteps outside, and Henri drew the door a little closer. But he was dismayed to find it Marie. She crept in, a white and broken thing, and looked about her.

"Maurice!" she called.

She sat down for a moment, and then, seeing the disorder about her, set to work to clear the table. It was then that Henri lowered his pistol and opened the door.

"Don't shriek, Marie," he said.

She turned and saw him, and clutched at the table.

"Monsieur!"

"Marie," he said quietly, "go up these stairs and remain quiet. Do not walk round. And do not come down, no matter what you hear!"

She obeyed him, stumbling somewhat. For she had seen his revolver, and it frightened her. But as she passed him she clutched at his sleeve.

"He is good-Maurice," she said, gasping. "Of the father I know nothing, but Maurice —"

"Go up and be silent!" was all he said.

Now, by all that goes to make a story, Sara Lee should have met Mabel at the Hôtel des Arcades in Dunkirk, and should have been able to make that efficient young woman burn with jealousy-Mabel, who from the safety of her hospital in Boulogne considered Dunkirk the Front.

Indeed Sara Lee, to whom the world was beginning to seem very small, had had some such faint hope. But Mabel was not there, and it was not until long after that they met at all, and then only when the lights had gone down and Sara Lee was again knitting by the fire.

There were a few nurses there, in their white veils with the red cross over the forehead, and one or two Englishwomen in hats that sat a trifle too high on the tops of their heads and with long lists before them which they checked as they ate. Aviators in leather coats; a few Spahis in cloak and turban, with full-gathered bloomers and high boots; some American ambulance drivers, rather noisy and very young; and many officers, in every uniform of the Allied armies-sat at food together and for a time forgot their anxieties under the influence of lights, food and warmth, and red and white wine mixed with water.

When he chose, Jean could be a delightful companion; not with Henri's lift of spirits, but quietly interesting. And that evening he was a new Jean to Sara Lee, a man of the world, talking of world affairs. He found her apt and intelligent, and for Sara Lee much that had been clouded cleared up forever that night. Until then she had known only the humanities of the war, or its inhumanities. There, over that little table, she learned something of its politics and its inevitability. She had been working in the dark, with her heart only. Now she began to grasp the real significance of it all, of Belgium's anxiety for many years, of Germany's cold and cruel preparation, and empty protests of friendship. She learned of the flight of the government from Brussels, the most important state papers being taken away in a hand cart, on top of which, at the last moment, some flustered official had placed a tall silk hat! She learned of the failure of great fortifications before the invaders' heavy guns. And he had drawn for her such a picture of Albert of Belgium as she was never to forget.

Perhaps Sara Lee's real growth began that night, over that simple dinner at the Hôtel des Arcades.

"I wish," she said at last, "that Uncle James could have heard all this. He was always so puzzled about it all. And-you make it so clear."

When dinner was over a bit of tension had relaxed in her somewhat. She had been too close, for too long. And when a group of Belgian officers, learning who she was, asked to be presented and gravely thanked her, she flushed with happiness.

"We must see if mademoiselle shall not have a medal," said the only one who spoke English.

"A medal? For what?"

"For courage," he said, bowing. "Belgium has little to give, but it can at least do honor to a brave lady."

Jean was smiling when they passed on. What a story would this slip of a girl take home with her!

But: "I don't think I want a medal, Jean," she said. "I didn't come for that. And after all it is you and Henri who have done the thing-not I."

Accustomed to women of a more sophisticated class, Jean had at first taken her naïveté for the height of subtlety. He was always expecting her to betray herself. But after that evening with her he changed. Just such simplicity had been his wife's. Sometimes Sara Lee reminded him of her-the upraising of her eyes or an unstudied gesture.

He sighed.

"You are very wonderful, you Americans," he said. It was the nearest to a compliment that he had ever come. And after that evening he was always very gentle with her. Once he had protected her because Henri had asked him to do so; now he himself became in his silent way her protector.

The ride home through the dark was very quiet. Sara Lee sat beside him watching the stars and growing increasingly anxious as they went, not too rapidly, toward the little house. There were no lights. Air raids had grown common in Dunkirk, and there were no street lights in the little city. Once on the highway Jean lighted the lamps, but left them very low, and two miles from the little house he put them out altogether. They traveled by starlight then, following as best they could the tall trees that marked the road. Now and then they went astray at that, and once they tilted into the ditch and had hard pulling to get out.

At the top of the street Jean stopped and went on foot a little way down. He came back, with the report that new shells had made the way impassable; and again Sara Lee shivered. If the little house was gone!

But it was there, and lighted too. Through its broken shutters came the yellow glow of the oil lamp that now hung over the table in the *salle à manger*.

Whatever Jean's anxieties had been fell from him as he pushed open the door. Henri's voice was the first thing they heard. He was too much occupied to notice their approach.

So it was that Sara Lee saw, for the last time, the miller and his son, Maurice; saw them, but did not know them, for over their heads were bags of their own sacking, with eyeholes roughly cut in them. Their hands were bound, and three soldiers were waiting to take them away.

"I have covered your heads," Henri was saying in French, "because it is not well that our brave Belgians should know that they have been betrayed by those of their own number."

It was a cold and terrible Henri who spoke.

"Take them away," he said to the waiting men.

A few moments later he turned from the door and heard Sara Lee sobbing in her room. He tapped, and on receiving no reply he went in. The room was unharmed, and by the light of a candle he saw the girl, face down on the bed. He spoke to her, but she only lay crouched deeper, her shoulders shaking.

"It is war, mademoiselle," he said, and went closer. Then suddenly all the hurt of the past days, all the bitterness of the last hour, were lost in an overwhelming burst of tenderness.

He bent over her and put his arms round her.

"That I should have hurt you so!" he said softly. "I, who would die for you, mademoiselle. I who worship you." He buried his face in the warm hollow of her neck and held her close. He was trembling. "I love you," he whispered. "I love you."

She quieted under his touch. He was very strong, and there was refuge in his arms. For a moment she lay still, happier than she had been for weeks. It was Henri who was shaken now and the girl who was still.

But very soon came the thing that, after all, he expected. She drew herself away from him, and Henri, sensitive to every gesture, stood back.

"Who are they?" was the first thing she said. It rather stabbed him. He had just told her that he loved her, and never before in his careless young life had he said that to any woman.

"Spies," he said briefly.

A flushed and tearful Sara Lee stood up then and looked up at him gravely.

"Then-that is what you do?"

"Yes, mademoiselle."

Quite suddenly she went to him and held up her face.

"Please kiss me, Henri," she said very simply. "I have been cruel and stupid, and —"

But he had her in his arms then, and he drew her close as though he would never let her go. He was one great burst of joy, poor Henri. But when she gently freed herself at last it was to deliver what seemed for a time his death wound.

"You have paid me a great tribute," she said, still simply and gravely. "I wanted you to kiss me, because of what you said. But that will have to be all, Henri dear."

"All?" he said blankly.

"You haven't forgotten, have you? I —I am engaged to somebody else."

Henri stood still, swaying a little.

"And you love him? More than you care for me?"

"He is-he is my kind," said Sara Lee rather pitifully. "I am not what you think me. You see me here, doing what you think is good work, and you are grateful. And you don't see any other women. So I —"

"And you think I love you because I see no one else?" he demanded, still rather stunned.

"Isn't that part of it?"

He flung out his hands as though he despaired of making her understand.

"This man at home —" he said bitterly; "this man who loves you so well that he let you cross the sea and come here alone-do you love him very dearly?"

"I am promised to him."

All at once Sara Lee saw the little parlor at home, and Harvey, gentle, rather stolid and dependable. Oh, very dependable. She saw him as he had looked the night he had said he loved her, rather wistful and very, very tender. She could not hurt him so. She had said she was going back to him, and she must go.

"I love him very much, Henri."

Very quietly, considering the hell that was raging in him, Henri bent over and kissed her hand. Then he turned it over, and for an instant he held his cheek against its warmth. He went out at once, and Sara Lee heard the door slam.

XVI

Time passed quickly, as always it does when there is work to do. Round the ruined houses the gray grass turned green again, and in travesties of gardens early spring flowers began to show a touch of color.

The first of them greeted Sara Lee one morning as she stood on her doorstep in the early sun. She gathered them and placed them, one on each grave, in the cemetery near the poplar trees, where small wooden crosses, sometimes surmounted by a cap, marked many graves.

Marie, a silent subdued Marie, worked steadily in the little house. She did not weep, but now and then Sara Lee found her stirring something on the stove and looking toward the quiet mill in the fields. And once Sara Lee, surprising that look on her face, put her arms about the girl and held her for a moment. But she did not say anything. There was nothing to say.

With the opening up of the spring came increased movement and activity among the troops. The beach and the sand dunes round La Panne were filled with drilling men, Belgium's new army. Veterans of the winter, at rest behind the lines, sat in the sun and pared potatoes for the midday meal. Convalescents from the hospital appeared in motley garments from the Ambulance Ocean and walked along the water front, where the sea, no longer gray and sullen, rolled up in thin white lines of foam to their very feet. Winter straw came out of wooden sabots. Winter-bitten hands turned soft. Canal boats blossomed out with great washings. And the sentry at the gun emplacement in the sand up the beach gave over gathering sticks for his fire, and lay, when no one was about, in a hollow in the dune, face to the sky.

So spring came to that small fragment of Belgium which had been saved, spring and hope. Soon now the great and powerful Allies would drive out the Huns, and all would be as it had been. Splendid rumors were about. The Germans were already yielding at La Bassée. There was to be a great drive along the entire Front, and hopefully one would return home in time for the spring planting.

A sort of informal council took place occasionally in the little house. Maps replaced the dressings on the table in the *salle à manger*, and junior officers, armed with Sara Lee's box of pins, thrust back the enemy at various points and proved conclusively that his position was untenable. They celebrated these paper victories with Sara Lee's tea, and went away the better for an hour or so of hope and tea and a girl's soft voice and quiet eyes.

Now and then there was one, of course, who lagged behind his fellows, with a yearning tenderness in his face that a glance from the girl would have quickly turned to love. But Sara Lee had no coquetry. When, as occasionally happened, there was a bit too much fervor when her hand was kissed, she laid it where it belonged-to loneliness and the spring-and became extremely maternal and very, very kind. Which-both of them-are death blows to young love.

The winter floods were receding. Along the Yser Canal mud-caked flats began to appear, with here and there rusty tangles of barbed wire. And with the lessening of the flood came new activities to the little house. The spring drive was coming.

There was spring indeed, everywhere but in Henri's heart.

Day after day messages were left with Sara Lee by men in uniform-sometimes letters, sometimes a word. And these she faithfully cared for until such time as Jean came for them. Now and then it was Henri who came, but when he stayed in the village he made his headquarters at the house of the mill. There, with sacking over the windows, he wrote his reports by lamplight, reports which Jean carried back to the villa in the fishing village by the sea.

However, though he no longer came and went as before, Henri made frequent calls at the house of mercy. But now he came in the evenings, when the place was full of men. Sara Lee was doing more dressings than before. The semi-armistice of winter was over, and there were nights when a row of wounded men lay on the floor in the little *salle à manger* and waited, in a sort of dreadful quiet, to be taken away.

Rumors came of hard fighting farther along the line, and sometimes, on nights when the clouds hung low, the flashes of the guns at Ypres looked like incessant lightning. From the sand dunes at Nieuport and Dixmude there was firing also, and the air seemed sometimes to be full of scouting planes.

The Canadians were moving toward the Front at Neuve Chapelle at that time. And one day a lorry, piled high with boxes, rolled and thumped down the street, and halted by René.

"Rather think we are lost," explained the driver, grinning sheepishly at René.

There were four boys in khaki on the truck, and not a word of French among them. Sara Lee, who rolled her own bandages now, heard the speech and came out.

"Good gracious!" she said, and gave an alarmed glance at the sky. But it was the noon hour, when every good German abandons war for food, and the sky was empty.

The boys cheered perceptibly. Here was at last some one who spoke a Christian tongue.

"Must have taken the wrong turning, miss," said one of them, saluting.

"Where do you want to go?" she asked. "You are very close to the Belgian Front here. It is not at all safe."

They all saluted; then, staring at her curiously, told her.

"Dear me!" said Sara Lee. "You are a long way off. And a long way from home too."

They smiled. They looked, with their clean-shaven faces, absurdly young after the bearded Belgian soldiers.

"I am an American, too," said Sara Lee with just a touch of homesickness in her voice. She had been feeling lonely lately. "If you have time to come in I could give you luncheon. René can tell us if any German air machines come over."

Would they come in? Indeed, yes! They crawled down off the lorry, and took off their caps, and ate every particle of food in the house. And, though they were mutely curious at first, soon they were asking questions. How long had she been there? What did she do? Wasn't it dangerous?

"Not so dangerous as it looks," said Sara Lee, smiling. "The Germans seldom bother the town now. It is not worth while."

Later on they went over the house. They climbed the broken staircase and stared toward the break in the poplar trees, from the roofless floor above.

"Some girl!" one of them said in an undertone.

The others were gazing intently toward the Front. Never before had they been so close. Never had they seen a ruined town. War, until now, had been a thing of Valcartier, of a long voyage, of much drill in the mud at Salisbury Plain. Now here they saw, at their feet, what war could do.

"Damn them!" said one of the boys suddenly. "Fellows, we'll get back at them soon."

So they went away, a trifle silent and very grateful. But before they left they had a glimpse of Sara Lee's room, with the corner gone, and Harvey's picture on the mantel.

"Some girl!" they repeated as they drove up the street. It was the tribute of inarticulate youth.

Sara Lee went back to her bandages and her thoughts. She had not a great deal of time to think, what with the officers stopping in to fight their paper-and-pin battles, and with letters to write and dressings to make and supplies to order. She began to have many visitors-officers from the French lines, correspondents on tours of the Front, and once even an English cabinet member, who took six precious lumps of sugar in his tea and dug a piece of shell out of the wall with his pocketknife as a souvenir.

Once a British aviator brought his machine down in the field by the mill, and walked over with the stiff stride of a man who has been for hours in the air. She gave him tea and bread and butter, and she learned then of the big fighting that was to come.

When she was alone she thought about Henri. Generally her thoughts were tender; always they were grateful. But she was greatly puzzled. He had said that he loved her. Then, if he loved her, why should he not be gentle and kind to her? Men did not hurt the women they loved. And because she was hurt, she was rather less than just. He had not asked her to marry him. He had said that he loved her, but that was different. And the insidious poison of Harvey's letter about foreigners began to have its effect.

The truth was that she was tired. The strain was telling on her. And at a time when she needed every moral support Henri had drawn off behind a wall of misery, and all her efforts at a renewal of their old friendship only brought up against a sort of stony despair.

There were times, too, when she grew a little frightened. She was so alone. What if Henri went away altogether? What if he took away the little car, and his protection, and the supplies that came so regularly? It was not a selfish fear. It was for her work that she trembled.

For the first time she realized her complete dependence on his good will. And now and then she felt that it would be good to see Harvey again, and be safe from all worry, and not have to depend on a man who loved her as Henri did. For that she never doubted. Inexperienced as she was in such matters, she knew that the boy loved her. Just how wildly she did not know until later, too late to undo what the madness had done.

Then one day a strange thing happened. It had been raining, and when in the late afternoon the sun came out it gleamed in the puddles that filled the shell holes in the road and set to a red blaze the windows of the house of the mill.

First, soaring overhead, came a half dozen friendly planes. Next, the eyes of the enemy having thus been blinded, so to speak, there came a regiment of fresh troops, swinging down the street for all the world as though the German Army was safely drinking beer in Munich. They passed René, standing open-mouthed in the doorway, and one wag of a Belgian boy, out of sheer joy of spring, did the goose step as he passed the little sentry and, head screwed round in the German salute, crossed his eyes over his impudent nose.

Came, then, the planes. Came the regiment, which turned off into a field and there spread itself, like a snake uncoiling, into a double line. Came a machine, gray and battered, containing officers. Came a general with gold braid on his shoulder, and a pleasant smile. Came the strange event.

The general found Sara Lee in the *salle à manger* cutting cotton into three-inch squares, and he stood in the doorway and bowed profoundly.

"Mademoiselle Kennedy?" he inquired.

Sara Lee replied to that, and then gave a quick thought to her larder. Because generals usually meant tea. But this time at last, Sara Lee was to receive something, not to give. She turned very white when she was told, and said she had not deserved it; she was indeed on the verge of declining, not knowing that there are certain things one does not decline. But Marie brought her hat and jacket —a smiling, tremulous Marie-and Sara Lee put them on.

The general was very tall. In her short skirt and with flying hair she looked like a child beside him as they walked across the fields. Suddenly Sara Lee was terribly afraid she was going to cry.

The troops stood rigidly at attention. And a cold wind flapped Sara Lee's skirts, and the guns hammered at Ypres, and the general blew on his fingers. And soon a low open car came down the street and the King got out. Sara Lee watched him coming-his tall, slightly stooped figure, his fair hair, his plain blue uniform. Sara Lee had never seen a king before, and she had always thought of them as sitting up on a sort of platform-never as trudging through spring mud.

"What shall I do?" she asked nervously.

"He will shake hands, mademoiselle. Bow as he approaches. That is all."

The amazing interlude, indeed! With Sara Lee being decorated by the King, and troops drawn up to do her honor, and over all the rumbling of the great guns. A palpitating and dazed Sara Lee, when the decoration was fastened to her black jacket, a Sara Lee whose hat blew off at exactly the worst moment and rolled, end on, like a hoop, into a puddle.

But, oddly, she did not mind about the hat. She had only one conscious thought just then. She hoped that, wherever Uncle James might be in that world of the gone before, he might know what was happening to her-or even see it. He would have liked it. He had believed in the Belgians and in the King. And now-the King did not go at once. He went back to the little house and went through it. And he and one of his generals climbed to the upper floor, and the King stood looking out silently toward the land he loved and which for a time was no longer his.

He came down after a time, stooping his tall figure in the low doorway, and said he would like some tea. So Marie put the kettle on, and Sara Lee and the King talked. It was all rather dazing. Every now and then she forgot certain instructions whispered her by the general, and after a time the King said: "Why do you do that, mademoiselle?"

For Sara Lee, with an intent face and moving lips, had been stepping backward.

Sara Lee flushed to the eyes.

"Because, sire, I was told to remain at a distance of six feet."

"But we are being informal," said the King, smiling. "And it is a very little room."

Sara Lee, who had been taught in the schoolroom that kings are usurpers of the divine rights of the people-Sara Lee lost just a bit of her staunch democracy that day. She saw the King of the Belgians for what he really was, a ruler, but a symbol as well. He represented his country, as the Flag she loved represented hers. The flag was America, the King was Belgium. That was all.

It was a very humble and flushed Sara Lee who watched the gray car go flying up the street later on. She went in and told the whole story to Harvey's picture, but it was difficult to feel that he was hearing. His eyes were turned away and his face was set and stern. And, at last, she gave it up. This thing which meant so much to her would never mean anything to Harvey. She knew, even then, what he would say.

"Decorate you! I should think they might. Medals are cheap. Everybody over there is getting medals. You feed their men and risk your life and your reputation, and they give you a thing to pin on. It's cheap at the price."

And later on those were Harvey's very words. But to be fair to him they were but the sloughing of a wound that would not heal.

That evening Henri came again. He was, for the first time, his gay self again-at least on the surface. It was as though, knowing what he was going into, he would leave with Sara Lee no feeling, if he never returned, that she had inflicted a lasting hurt. He was everywhere in the little house, elbowing his way among the men with his cheery nonsense, bantering the weary ones until they smiled, carrying hot water for Sara Lee and helping her now and then with a bad dressing.

"If you would do it in this fashion, mademoiselle," he would say, "with one turn of the bandage over the elbow —"

"But it won't hold that way."

"You say that to me, mademoiselle? I who have taught you all you know of bandaging?"

They would wrangle a bit, and end by doing it in Sara Lee's way.

He had a fund of nonsense that he drew on, too, when a dressing was painful. It would run like this, to an early accompaniment of groans:

"Pierre, what can you put in your left hand that you cannot place in the right? Stop grunting like a pig, and think, man!"

Pierre would give a final rumble and begin to think deeply.

"I cannot think. I—in my left hand, *monsieur le capitaine?*"

"In your left hand."

The little crowd in the dressing room would draw in close about the table to listen.

"I do not know, monsieur."

"Idiot!" Henri would say. "Your right elbow, man!"

And the dressing was done.

He had an inexhaustible stock of such riddles, almost never guessed. He would tell the answer and then laugh delightedly. And pain seemed to leave the little room when he entered it.

It was that night that Henri disappeared.

XVII

There was a question to settle, and it was for Henri to do it. Two questions indeed. One was a matter of engineering, and before the bottom fell out of his world Henri had studied engineering. The second was more serious.

For the first, this thing had happened. Of all the trenches to be held, the Belgians had undeniably the worst. Properly speaking they were not trenches at all, but shallow gutters dug a foot or two into the saturated ground and then built man-high with bags of earth or sand. Here and there they were not dug at all, but were purely shelters, against a railway embankment, of planks or sandbags, and reinforced by rails from the deserted track behind which they were hidden.

For this corner of Belgium had been saved by turning it into a shallow lake. By opening the gates in the dikes the Allies had let in the sea and placed a flood in front of the advancing enemy. The battle front was a reeking pond. The opposing armies lived like duck hunters in a swamp. To dig a foot was to encounter water. Machine guns here and there sat but six inches above the yellow flood. Men lay in pools to fire them. To reach outposts were narrow paths built first of bags of earth —a life, sometimes for every bag. And, when this filling was sufficient, on top a path of fascines, bound together in bundles, made a footway.

For this reason the Belgians approached their trenches not through deep cuts which gave them shelter but with no other cover than the darkness of night. During the day, they lay in their shallow dugouts, cut off from any connection with the world behind them. Food, cooked miles away, came up at night, cold and unappetizing. For water, having exhausted their canteens, there was nothing but the brackish tide before them, ill-smelling and reeking of fever. Water carts trundled forward at night, but often they were far too few.

The Belgians, having faced their future through long years of anxiety, had been trained to fight. In a way they had been trained to fight a losing war, for they could not hope to defeat their greedy neighbor on the east. But now they found themselves fighting almost not at all, condemned to inactivity, to being almost passively slaughtered by enemy artillery, and to living under such conditions as would have sapped the courage of a less desperate people.

To add to the difficulties, not only did the sea encroach, turning a fertile land into a salt marsh, but the winter rains, unusually heavy that tragic first winter, and lacking their usual egress to the sea, spread the flood. There were many places well back of the lines where fields were flooded, and where roads, sadly needed, lost themselves in unfordable wallows of mud and water.

Henri then, knowing all this-none better-had his first question to settle, which was this: As spring advanced the flood had commenced to recede. Time came when, in those trenches now huddled shallow behind the railway track, one could live in a certain comfort. In the deeper ones, the bottom of the trench appeared for the first time.

On a day previous, however, the water had commenced to come back. There had been no rain, but little by little in a certain place yellow, ill-smelling little streams began to flow sluggishly into the trenches. Seeped, rather than flowed. At first the Belgian officers laid it to that bad luck that had so persistently pursued them. Then they held a conference in the small brick house with its maps and its pine tables and its picture of an American harvester on the wall, which was now headquarters.

Sitting under the hanging lamp, with an orderly making coffee at a stove in the corner, they talked it over. Henri was there, silent before his elders, but intently listening. And at last they turned to him.

"I can go and find out," he said quietly. "It is possible, though I do not see how." He smiled. "They are, I think, only drying themselves at our expense. It is a bit of German humor."

But the cry of "Calais in a month!" was in the air, and undoubtedly there had been renewed activity along the German Front near the sea. The second question to be answered was dependent on the first.

Had the Germans, as Henri said, merely shifted the water, by some clever engineering, to the Belgian trenches, or was there some bigger thing on hand? What, for instance, if they were about to attempt to drain the inundation, smash the Belgian line, and march by the Dunkirk road to Calais?

So, that night while Henri jested about Pierre's right elbow and watched Sara Lee for a smile, he had difficult work before him.

Sometime near midnight he slipped away. Jean was waiting in the street, and wrung the boy's hand.

"I could go with you," he said rather wistfully.

"You don't speak their ugly tongue."

"I could be mute-shell shock. You could be helping me back."

But Henri only held his hand a moment and shook his head.

"You would double the risk, and-what good would it do?"

"Two pistols are better than one."

"I have two pistols, my friend," said Henri, and turned the corner of the building, past the boards René had built in, toward the house of the mill. But once out of Jean's sight he stopped a moment, his hand resting against that frail wall to Sara Lee's room. It was his good-by to her.

For three days Jean stayed in the village. He slept at the mill, but he came for his meals to the little house. Once he went to Dunkirk and brought out provisions and the mail, including Sara Lee's monthly allowance. But mostly he sat in the mill house and waited. He could not read.

"You do not eat at all, Jean," Sara Lee said to him more than once. And twice she insisted that he was feverish, and placed a hand that was somewhat marred with much peeling of vegetables, on his forehead.

"I am entirely well, mademoiselle," he would say, and draw back. He had anxieties enough just now without being reminded by the touch of a woman's hand of all that he had lost.

Long before that Sara Lee had learned not to question Jean about Henri's absences. Even his knowledge, now, that she knew something of Henri's work, did not remove the barrier. So Sara Lee waited, as did Jean, but more helplessly. She knew something was wrong, but she had not Jean's privilege of going at night to the trenches and there waiting, staring over the gray water with its ugly floating shadows, for Henri to emerge from the flood.

Something rather forced and mechanical there was those days in her work. Her smile was rather set. She did not sleep well. And one night she violated Henri's orders and walked across the softened fields to beyond the poplar trees.

There was nothing to see except an intermittent flash from the clouds that hung low over the sea at Nieuport, where British gunboats were bombarding the coast; or the steady streaks from the Ypres salient, where night and day the guns never rested.

From the Belgian trenches, fifteen hundred feet or so away, there was no sound. A German electric signal blazed its message in code, and went out quickly. Now and then a rifle shot, thin and sharp, rang out from where, under the floating starlights, keen eyes on each side watched for movements on the other.

Sara Lee sat down under a tree and watched for a while. Then she found herself crying softly. It was all so sad, and useless, and cruel. And somewhere there ahead was Henri, Henri with his blue eyes, his smile, the ardor of his young arms-Henri, who had been to her many friends.

Sara Lee had never deceived herself about Henri. She loved him. But she was quite certain she was not in love with him, which is entirely different. She knew that this last was impossible, because she was engaged to Harvey. What was probably the truth was that she loved them both in entirely different ways. Men have always insisted on such possibilities, and have even asserted their right, now and then, to love two women at the same time. But women are less frank with themselves.

And, in such cases, there is no grand passion. There are tenderness, and the joy of companionship, and sometimes a touching dependence. But it is not a love that burns with a white fire.

Perhaps Sara Lee was one of those women who are always loved more than they love. There are such women, not selfish, not seeking love, but softly feminine, kind, appealing and genuine. Men need, after all, but an altar on which to lay tribute. And the high, remote white altar that was Sara Lee had already received the love of two strong men.

She was not troubling her head that night, however, about being an altar, of a sort. She cried a little at first, because she was terrified for Henri and because Jean's face was growing pinched and gray. Then she cried very hard, prone on the ground and face down, because Henri was young, and all of life should have been before him. And he was missing.

Henri was undeniably missing. Even the King knew it now, and set down in his heart, among the other crosses there, Henri's full name, which we may not know, and took to pacing his little study and looking out at the spring sea.

That night Marie, having ladled to the bottom of her kettle, found Sara Lee missing, and was told by René of the direction she had taken. Marie, muttering to herself, set out to find her, and almost stumbled over her in the wood by the road.

She sat down on the ground without a word and placed a clumsy hand on the girl's shoulder. It was not until Sara Lee ceased sobbing that she spoke:

"It is far from hopeless, mademoiselle."

They had by now established a system of communication. Sara Lee spoke her orders in halting French, but general conversation was beyond her. And much hearing of English had taught the Belgian girl enough to follow.

Sara Lee replied, then, in smothered English:

"He is gone, Marie. He will never come back."

"Who can tell? There are many missing who are not dead."

Sara Lee shuddered. For spies were not made prisoners. They had no rights as prisoners of war. Their own governments did not protect them. To Henri capture was death. But she could not say this to Marie.

Marie sat softly stroking Sara Lee's hair, her own eyes tragic and tearless.

"Even if it were-the other," she said, "it is not so bad to die for one's country. The thing that is terrible, that leaves behind it only bitterness and grief and no hope, mademoiselle, even with many prayers, is that one has died a traitor."

She coaxed Sara Lee back at last. They went through the fields, for fresh troops were being thrown into the Belgian trenches and the street was full of men. Great dray horses were dragging forward batteries, the heavy guns sliding and slipping In the absence of such information as only Henri had been wont to bring it was best to provide for the worst.

The next day Jean did not come over for breakfast, and René handed Sara Lee a note.

"I am going to England," Jean had written that dawn in the house of the mill. "And from there to Holland. I can get past the barrier and shall work down toward the Front. I must learn what has happened, mademoiselle. As you know, if he was captured, there is no hope. But there is an excellent chance that he is in hiding, unable to get back. Look for me in two weeks."

There followed what instructions he had given as to her supplies, which would come as before. Beautifully written in Jean's small fine hand, it spelled for Sara Lee the last hope. She read Jean's desperation through its forced cheerfulness. And she faced for the first time a long period of loneliness in the crowded little house.

She tried very hard to fill the gap that Henri had left-tried to joke with the men in her queer bits of French; was more smiling than ever, for fear she might be less. But now and then in cautious whispers she heard Henri's name, and her heart contracted with very terror.

A week. Two weeks. Twice the village was bombarded severely, but the little house escaped by a miracle. Marie considered it the same miracle that left holy pictures unhurt on the walls of destroyed houses, and allowed the frailest of old ebony and rosewood crucifixes to remain unharmed.

Great generals, often as tall as they were great, stopped at the little house to implore Sara Lee to leave. But she only shook her head.

"Not unless you send me away," she always said; "and that would break my heart."

"But to move, mademoiselle, only to the next village!" they would remonstrate, and as a final argument: "You are too valuable to risk an injury."

"I must remain here," she said. And some of them thought they understood. When an unusually obdurate officer came along, Sara Lee would insist on taking him to the cellar.

"You see!" she would say, holding her candle high. "It is a nice cellar, warm and dry. It is" —proudly —"one of the best cellars in the village. It is a really homelike cellar."

The officer would go away then, and send her cigarettes for her men or, as in more than one case, a squad with bags of earth and other things to protect the little house as much as possible. After a time the little house began to represent the ideas in protection and camouflage, then in its early stages, of many different minds.

René shot a man there one night, a skulking figure working its way in the shadows up the street. It was just before dawn, and René, who was sleepless those days, like the others, called to him. The man started to run, dodging behind walls. But René ran faster and killed him.

He was a German in Belgian peasant's clothing. But he wore the great shoes of the German soldier, and he had been making a rough map of the Belgian trenches.

Sara Lee did not see him. But when she heard the shot she went out, and René told her breathlessly.

From that time on her terrors took the definite form of Henri lying dead in a ruined street, and being buried, as this man was buried, without ceremony and without a prayer, in some sodden spring field.

XVIII

As the spring advanced Harvey grew increasingly bitter; grew morbid and increasingly self-conscious also. He began to think that people were smiling behind his back, and when they asked about Sara Lee he met with almost insulting brevity what he felt was half-contemptuous kindness. He went nowhere, and worked all day and until late in the night. He did well in his business, however, and late in March he received a substantial raise in salary. He took it without enthusiasm, and told Belle that night at dinner with apathy.

After the evening meal it was now his custom to go to his room and there, shut in, to read. He read no books on the war, and even the quarter column entitled Salient Points of the Day's War News hardly received a glance from him now.

In the office when the talk turned to the war, as it did almost hourly, he would go out or scowl over his letters.

"Harvey's hit hard," they said there.

"He's acting like a rotten cub," was likely to be the next sentence. But sometimes it was: "Well, what'd you expect? Everything ready to get married, and the girl beating it for France without notice! I'd be sore myself."

On the day of the raise in salary his sister got the children to bed and straightened up the litter of small garments that seemed always to bestrew the house, even to the lower floor. Then she went into Harvey's room. Coat and collar off, he was lying on the bed, but not reading. His book lay beside him, and with his arms under his head he was staring at the ceiling.

She did not sit down beside him on the bed. They were an undemonstrative family, and such endearments as Belle used were lavished on her children. But her eyes were kind, and a little nervous.

"Do you mind talking a little, Harvey?"

"I don't feel like talking much. I'm tired, I guess. But go on. What is it? Bills?"

She came to him in her constant financial anxieties, and always he was ready to help her out. But his tone now was gruff. A slight flush of resentment colored her cheeks.

"Not this time, Harve. I was just thinking about things."

"Sit down."

She sat on the straight chair beside the bed, the chair on which, in neat order, Harvey placed his clothing at night, his shoes beneath, his coat over the back.

"I wish you'd go out more, Harvey."

"Why? Go out and talk to a lot of driveling fools who don't care for me any more than I do for them?"

"That's not like you, Harve."

"Sorry." His tone softened. "I don't care much about going round, Belle. That's all. I guess you know why."

"So does everybody else."

He sat up and looked at her.

"Well, suppose they do? I can't help that, can I? When a fellow has been jilted —"

"You haven't been jilted."

He lay down again, his arms under his head; and Belle knew that his eyes were on Sara Lee's picture on his dresser.

"It amounts to the same thing."

"Harvey," Belle said hesitatingly, "I've brought Sara Lee's report from the Ladies' Aid. May I read it to you?"

"I don't want to hear it." Then: "Give it here. I'll look at it."

He read it carefully, his hands rather unsteady. So many men given soup, so many given chocolate. So many dressings done. And at the bottom Sara Lee's request for more money-an apologetic, rather breathless request, and closing, rather primly with this:

"I am sure that the society will feel, from the above report, that the work is worth while, and worth continuing. I am only sorry that I cannot send photographs of the men who come for aid, but as they come at night it is impossible. I enclose, however, a small picture of the house, which is now known as the little house of mercy."

"At night!" said Harvey. "So she's there alone with a lot of ignorant foreigners at night. Why the devil don't they come in the daytime?"

"Here's the picture, Harvey."

He got up then, and carried the tiny photograph over close to the gas jet. There he stood for a long time, gazing at it. There was René with his rifle and his smile. There was Marie in her white apron. And in the center, the wind blowing her soft hair, was Sara Lee.

Harvey groaned and Belle came over and putting her hand on his shoulder looked at the photograph with him.

"Do you know what I think, Harvey?" she said. "I think Sara Lee is right and you are wrong."

He turned on her almost savagely.

"That's not the point!" he snapped out. "I don't begrudge the poor devils their soup. What I feel is this: If she'd cared a tinker's damn for me she'd never have gone. That's all."

He returned to a moody survey of the picture.

"Look at it!" he said. "She insists that she's safe. But that fellow's got a gun. What for, if she's so safe? And look at that house! There's a corner shot away; and it's got no upper floor. Safe!"

Belle held out her hand.

"I must return the picture to the society, Harve."

"Not just yet," he said ominously. "I want to look at it. I haven't got it all yet. And I'll return it myself-with a short speech."

"Harvey!"

"Well," he retorted, "why shouldn't I tell that lot of old scandalmongers what I think of them? They'll sit here safe at home and beg money-God, one of them was in the office to-day! —and send a young girl over to-You'd better get out, Belle. I'm not company for any one to-night."

She turned away, but he came after her, and suddenly putting his arms round her he kissed her.

"Don't worry about me," he said. "I'm done with wearing my heart on my sleeve. She looks happy, so I guess I can be." He released her. "Good night. I'll return the picture."

He sat up very late, alternately reading the report and looking at the picture. It was unfortunate that Sara Lee had smiled into the camera. Coupled with her blowing hair it had given her a light-heartedness, a sort of joyousness, that hurt him to the soul.

He made some mad plans after he had turned out the lights-to flirt wildly with the unattached girls he knew; to go to France and confront Sara Lee and then bring her home. Or-He had found a way. He lay there and thought it over, and it bore the test of the broken sleep that followed. In the morning, dressing, he wondered he had not thought of it before. He was more cheerful at breakfast than he had been for weeks.

XIX

In the little house of mercy two weeks went by, and then a third. Soldiers marching out to the trenches sometimes wore flowers tucked gayly in their caps. More and more Allied aëroplanes were in the air. Sometimes, standing in the streets, Sara Lee saw one far overhead, while balloon-shaped clouds of bursting shells hung far below it.

Once or twice in the early morning a German plane, flying so low that one could easily see the black cross on each wing, reconnoitered the village for wagon trains or troops. Always they found it empty.

Hope had almost fled now. In the afternoons Marie went to the ruined church, and there knelt before the heap of marble and masonry that had once been the altar, and prayed. And Sara Lee, who had been brought up a Protestant and had never before entered a Catholic church, took to going there too. In some strange fashion the peace of former days seemed to cling to the little structure, roofless as it was. On quiet days its silence was deeper than elsewhere. On days of much firing the sound from within its broken walls seemed deadened, far away.

Marie burned a candle as she prayed, for that soul in purgatory which she had once loved, and now pitied. Sara Lee burned no candle, but she knelt, sometimes beside Marie, sometimes alone, and prayed for many things: that Henri should be living, somewhere; that the war might end; that that day there would be little wounding; that some day the Belgians might go home again; and that back in America Harvey might grow to understand and forgive her. And now and then she looked into the very depths of her soul, and on those days she prayed that her homeland might, before it was too late, see this thing as she was seeing it. The wanton waste of it all, the ghastly cruelty the Germans had brought into this war.

Sara Lee's vague thinking began to crystallize. This war was not a judgment sent from on high to a sinful world. It was the wicked imposition of one nation on other nations. It was national. It was almost racial. But most of all it was a war of hate on the German side. She had never believed in hate. There were ugly passions in the world-jealousy, envy, suspicion; but not hate. The word was not in her rather limited vocabulary.

There was no hate on the part of the men she knew. The officers who stopped in on their way to and from the trenches were gentlemen and soldiers. They were determined and grave; they resented, they even loathed. But they did not hate. The little Belgian soldiers were bewildered, puzzled, desperately resentful. But of hate, as translated into terms of frightfulness, they had no understanding.

Yet from the other side were coming methods of war so wantonly cruel, so useless save as inflicting needless agony, as only hate could devise. No strategic value justified them. They were spontaneous outgrowths of venom, nursed during the winter deadlock and now grown to full size and destructive power.

The rumor of a gas that seared and killed came to the little house as early as February. In March there came the first victims, poor writhing creatures, deprived of the boon of air, their seared lungs collapsed and agonized, their faces drawn into masks of suffering. Some of them died in the little house, and even after death their faces held the imprint of horror.

To Sara Lee, burying her own anxiety under the cloak of service, there came new and terrible thoughts. This was not war. The Germans had sent their clouds of poisoned gas across the inundation, but had made no attempt to follow. This was killing, for the lust of killing; suffering, for the joy of inflicting pain.

And a day or so later she heard of The Hague Convention. She had not known of it before. Now she learned of that gentlemen's agreement among nations, and that it said: "The use of poison or of poisoned weapons is forbidden." She pondered that carefully, trying to think dispassionately. Now and then she received a copy of a home newspaper, and she saw that the use of poison gases was being denied by Germans in America and set down to rumor and hysteria.

So, on a cold spring day, she sat down at the table in the *salle à manger* and wrote a letter to the President, beginning *"Dear Sir"*; and telling what she knew of poison gas. She also, on second thought, wrote one to Andrew Carnegie, who had built a library in her city. She felt that the expense to him of sending some one over to investigate would not be prohibitive, and something must be done.

She never heard from either of her letters, but she felt better for having written them. And a day or two later she received from Mrs. Travers, in England, a small supply of the first gas masks of the war. Simple and primitive they were, those first masks; useless, too, as it turned out —a square of folded gauze, soaked in some solution and then dried, with tapes to tie it over the mouth and nose. To adjust them the soldiers had but to stoop and wet them in the ever-present water in the trench, and then to tie them on.

Sara Lee gave them out that night, and there was much mirth in the little house, such mirth as there had not been since Henri went away. The Belgians called it a *bal masque*, and putting them on bowed before one another and requested dances, and even flirted coyly with each other over their bits of white gauze. And in the very middle of the gayety some one propounded one of Henri's idiotic riddles; and Sara Lee went across to her little room and closed the door and stood there with her eyes shut, for fear she would scream.

Then, one day, coming out of the little church, she saw the low broken gray car turn in at the top of the street and come slowly, so very slowly, toward her. There were two men in it.

One was Henri.

She ran, stumbling because of tears, up the street. It was Henri! There was no mistake. There he sat beside Jean, brushed and very neat; and very, very white.

"Mademoiselle!" he said, and came very close to crying himself when he saw her face. He was greatly excited. His sunken eyes devoured her as she ran toward him. Almost he held out his arms. But he could not do that, even if he would, for one was bandaged to his side.

It is rather sad to record how many times Sara Lee wept during her amazing interlude. For here is another time. She wept for joy and wretchedness. She stood on the running board and cried and smiled. And Jean winked his one eye rapidly.

"This idiot, mademoiselle," he said gruffly, "this maniac-he would not remain in Calais, with proper care. He must come on here. And rapidly. Could he have taken the wheel from me we should have been here an hour ago. But for once I have an advantage."

The car jolted to the little house, and Jean helped Henri out. Such a strange Henri, smiling and joyous, and walking at a crawl, even with Jean's support. He protested violently against being put to bed, and when he found himself led into Sara Lee's small room he openly rebelled.

"Never!" he said stubbornly, halting in the doorway. "This is mademoiselle's boudoir. Her drawing-room as well. I am going to the mill house and —"

He staggered.

So Sara Lee's room had a different occupant for a time, a thin and fine-worn young Belgian, who yielded to Sara Lee when Jean gave up in despair, and who proceeded, most unmanfully, to faint as soon as he was between the blankets.

If Sara Lee hoped to nurse Henri she was doomed to disappointment. Jean it was who took over the care of the boy, a Jean who now ate prodigiously, and whistled occasionally, and slept at night robed in his blanket on the floor beside Henri's bed, lest that rebellious invalid get up and try to move about.

On the first night, with the door closed, against Henri's entreaties, while the little house received its evening complement of men, and with Henri lying back on his pillows, fresh dressed as to the wounds in his arm and chest, fed with Sara Lee's daintiest, and resting, Jean found the boy's eyes resting on the mantel.

"Dear and obstinate friend," said Henri, "do you wish me to be happy?"

"You shall not leave the room or your bed. That is arranged for."

"How?" demanded Henri with interest.

"Because I have hidden away your trousers."

Henri laughed, but he sobered quickly.

"If you wish me to be happy," he said, "take away that American photograph. But first, please to bring it here."

Jean brought it, holding it gingerly between his thumb and forefinger. And Henri lay back and studied it.

"It is mademoiselle's fiancé," he said.

Jean grunted.

"Look at it, Jean," Henri said in his half-bantering tone, with despair beneath it; "and then look at me. Or no-remembering me as I was when I was a man. He is better, eh? It is a good face. But there is a jaw, a —Do you think he will be kind to her as she requires? She requires much kindness. Some women —"

He broke off and watched Jean anxiously.

"A half face!" Jean said scornfully. "The pretty view! As for kindness —" He put the photograph face down on the table. "I knew once a man in Belgium who married an American. At Antwerp. They were most unhappy."

Henri smiled.

"You are lying," he said with boyish pleasure in his own astuteness. "You knew no such couple. You are trying to make me resigned."

But quite a little later, when Jean thought he was asleep, he said: "I shall never be resigned."

So at last spring had come, and Henri and the great spring drive. The Germans had not drained the inundation, nor had they broken through to Calais. And it is not to be known here how much this utter failure had been due to the information Henri had secured before he was wounded.

One day in his bed Henri received a visit from the King, and was left lying with a decoration on his breast and a beatific, if somewhat sheepish, expression on his face. And one night the village was bombarded, and on Henri's refusing to be moved to the cellar Sara Lee took up a determined stand in his doorway, until at last he made a most humiliating move for safety.

Bit by bit Sara Lee got the story, its bare detail from Henri, its courage and sheer recklessness from Jean. It would, for instance, run like this, with Henri in a chair perhaps, and cutting dressings-since that might be done with one hand-and Sara Lee, sleeves rolled up and a great bowl of vegetables before her:

"And when you got through the water, Henri?" she would ask: "What then?"

"It was quite simple. They had put up some additional wire, however —"

"Where?"

"There was a break," he would explain. "I have told you-between their trenches. I had used it before to get through."

"But how could you go through?"

"Like a snake," he would say, smiling. "Very flat and wriggling. I have eaten of the dirt, mademoiselle."

Then he would stop and cut, very awkwardly, with his left hand.

"Go on," she would prompt him. "But they had put barbed wire there. Is that it? So you could not get through?"

"With tin cans on it, and stones in the cans. I thought I had removed them all, but there was one left. So they heard me."

More cutting and a muttered French expletive. Henri was not a particularly patient cripple. And apparently there was an end to the story.

"For goodness' sake," Sara Lee would exclaim despairingly; "so they heard you! That isn't all, is it?"

"It was almost all," he would say with his boyish smile.

"And they shot at you?"

"Even better. They shot me. That was this one." And he would point to his arm.

More silence, more cutting, a gathering exasperation on Sara Lee's part.

"Are you going on or not?"

"Then I pretended to be one of them, mademoiselle. I speak German as French. I pretended not to be hurt, but to be on a reconnoissance. And I got into the trench and we had a talk in the darkness. It was most interesting. Only if they had shown a light they would have seen that I was wounded."

By bits, not that day, but after many days, she got the story. In the next trench he slipped a sling over the wounded arm and, as a Bavarian on his way to the dressing station, got back.

"I had some trouble," he confessed one day. "Now and then one would offer to go back with me. And I did not care for assistance!"

But sometime later there was trouble. She was four days getting to that part of it. He had got behind the lines by that time, and he knew that in some way suspicion had been roused. He was weak by that time, and could not go far. He had lain hidden, for a day and part of a night, without water, in a destroyed barn, and then had escaped.

He got into the Belgian costume as before, but he could not wear a sling for his wounded arm. He got the peasant to thrust his helpless right hand into his pocket, and for two days he made a close inspection of what was going on. But fever had developed, and on the third night, half delirious, when he was spoken to by an officer he had replied, of all tongues, in English.

The officer shot him instantly in the chest. He fell and lay still and the officer bent over him. In that moment Henri stabbed him with a knife in his left hand. Men were coming from every direction, but he got away-he did not clearly remember how. And at dawn he fell into the Belgian farmhouse, apparently dying.

Jean's story, on the other hand, was given early and with no hesitation. He had crossed the border at Holland in civilian clothes, by the simple expedient of bribing a sentry. He had got, with little difficulty, to the farmhouse, and found Henri, now recovering but very weak; he was lying hidden in a garret, and he was suffering from hunger and lack of medical attention. In a wagon full of market stuff, Henri hidden in the bed of it, they had got to the border again. And there Jean had, it seemed, stabbed the sentry he had bribed before and driven on to neutral soil.

Not an unusual story, that of Henri and Jean. The journey across Belgium in the springless farm wagon was the worst. They had had to take roundabout lanes, avoiding the main highways. Fortunately, always at night there were friendly houses, kind hands to lift Henri into warm fire-lighted interiors. Many messages they had brought back, some of cheer, but too often of tragedy, from the small farmsteads of Belgium.

Then finally had been Holland, and the chartering of a boat-and at last —"Here we are, and here we are, and here we are again," sang Henri, chopping at his cotton and making a great show of cheerfulness before Sara Lee.

But with Jean sometimes he showed the black depression beneath. He would never be a man again. He was done for. He gained strength so slowly that he believed he was not gaining at all. He was not happy, and the unhappy mend slowly.

After the time he had asked Jean to take away Harvey's photograph he did not recur to the subject, but he did not need to. Jean knew, perhaps even better than Henri himself, that the boy was recklessly, hopelessly, not quite rationally in love with the American girl.

Also Henri was fretting about his work. Sometimes at night, following Henri's instructions, Jean wandered quietly along roads and paths that paralleled the Front. At such times his eyes were turned, not toward the trenches, but toward that flat country which lay behind, still dotted at that time with groves of trees, with canals overhung with pollard willows, and with here and there a farmhouse that at night took on in the starlight the appearance of being whole again.

Singularly white and peaceful were those small steadings of Belgium in the night hours-until cruel dawn showed them for what they were-skeletons of dead homes, clothed only at night with wraithlike roofs and chimneys; ghosts of houses, appearing between midnight and cock crow.

Jean had not Henri's eyes nor his recklessness nor his speed, for that matter. Now and then he saw the small appearing and disappearing lights on some small rise. He would reach the spot, with such shelter as possible, to find only a sugar-beet field, neglected and unplowed.

Then, one night, tragedy came to the little house of mercy.

XX

Harvey proceeded to put his plan into effect at once, with the simple method of an essentially simple nature. The thing had become intolerable; therefore it must end.

On the afternoon following his talk with Belle he came home at three o'clock. Belle heard him moving about in his room, and when she entered it, after he had gone, she found that he had shaved and put on his best suit.

She smiled a little. It was like Harvey to be literal. He had said he was going to go round and have a good time, and he was losing no time. But in their restricted social life, where most of the men worked until five o'clock or even later, there were fewer afternoon calls paid. Belle wondered with mild sisterly curiosity into what arena Harvey was about to fling his best hat.

But though Harvey paid a call that afternoon it was not on any of the young women he knew. He went to see Mrs. Gregory. She was at home-he had arranged for that by telephone-and the one butler of the neighborhood admitted him. It was a truculent young man, for all his politeness, who confronted Mrs. Gregory in her drawing-room —a quietly truculent young man, who came to the point while he was still shaking hands.

"You're not going to be glad to see me in a minute," he said in reply to her greeting.

"How can you know that?"

"Because I've come to get you to do something you won't want to do."

"We won't quarrel before we begin, then," she said pleasantly. "Because I really never do anything I don't wish to do."

But she gave him a second glance and her smile became a trifle forced. She knew all about Harvey and Sara Lee. She had heard rumors of his disapproval also. Though she was not a clever nor a very keen woman, she saw what was coming and braced herself for it.

Harvey had prepared in his mind a summary of his position, and he delivered it with the rapidity and strength of a blow.

"I know all about the Belgians, Mrs. Gregory," he said. "I'm sorry for them. So is every one, I suppose. But I want to know if you think a girl of twenty ought to be over there practically at the Front, and alone?" He gave her time to reply. "Would you like to have your daughter there, if you had one?"

"Perhaps not, under ordinary circumstances. But this is war."

"It is not our war."

"Humanity," said Mrs. Gregory, remembering the phrase she had written for a speech — "humanity has no nationality. It is of all men, for all men."

"That's men. Not women!"

He got up and stood on the hearthrug. He was singularly reminiscent of the time he had stood on Aunt Harriet's white fur rug and had told Sara Lee she could not go.

"Now see here, Mrs. Gregory," he said, "we'll stop beating about the bush, if you don't mind. She's got to come home. She's coming, if I have to go and get her!"

"You needn't look at me so fiercely. I didn't send her. It was her own idea."

Harvey sneered.

"No," he said slowly. "But I notice your society publishes her reports in the papers, and that the names of the officers are rarely missing."

Mrs. Gregory colored.

"We must have publicity to get money," she said. "It is hard to get. Sometimes I have had to make up the deficit out of my own pocket."

"Then for God's sake bring her home! If the thing has to go on, send over there some of the middle-aged women who have no ties. Let 'em get shot if they want to. They can write as good reports as she can, if that's all you want. And make as good soup," he added bitterly.

"It could be done, of course," she said, thoughtfully. "But — I must tell you this: I doubt if an older woman could have got where she has. There is no doubt that her charm, her youth and beauty have helped her greatly. We cannot —"

The very whites of his eyes turned red then. He shouted furiously that for their silly work and their love of publicity, they were trading on a girl's youth and beauty; that if anything happened to her he would publish the truth in every newspaper in the country; that they would at once recall Sara Lee or he would placard the city with what they were doing. These were only a few of the things he threw at her.

When he was out of breath he jerked the picture of the little house of mercy out of his pocket and flung it into her lap.

"There!" he said. "Do you know where that house is? It's in a ruined village. She hasn't said that, has she? Well, look at the masonry there. That's a shell hole in the street. That soldier's got a gun. Why? Because the Germans may march up that street any day on their way to Calais."

Mrs. Gregory looked at the picture. Sara Lee smiled into the sun. And René, ignorant that his single rifle was to oppose the march of the German Army to Calais-René smiled also.

Mrs. Gregory rose.

"I shall report your view to the society," she said coldly. "I understand how you feel, but I fail to see the reason for this attack on me."

"I guess you see all right!" he flung at her. "She's my future wife. If you hadn't put this nonsense into her head we'd be married now and she'd be here in God's country and not living with a lot of foreigners who don't know a good woman when they see one. I want her back, that's all. But I want her back safe. And if anything happens to her I'll make you pay-you and all your notoriety hunters."

He went out then, and was for leaving without his hat or coat, but the butler caught him at the door. Out in the spring sunlight he walked rapidly, still seething, remembering other bitter things he had meant to say, and repeating them to himself.

But he had said enough.

Mrs. Gregory's account of his visit she reported at a meeting specially called. The narrative lost nothing in the repetition. But the kindly women who sat in the church house sewing or knitting listened to what Harvey had said and looked troubled. They liked Sara Lee, and many of them had daughters of their own.

The photograph was passed around. Undoubtedly Sara Lee was living in a ruined village. Certainly ruined villages were only found very near the Front. And René unquestionably held a gun. Tales of German brutalities to women had come and were coming constantly to their ears. Mabel Andrews had written to them for supplies, and she had added to the chapter of horrors.

Briefly, the sense of the meeting was that Harvey had been brutal, but that he was right. An older woman in a safe place they might continue to support, but none of them would assume the responsibility of the crushing out of a young girl's life.

To be quite frank, possibly Harvey's appeal would have carried less weight had it not coincided with Sara Lee's request for more money. Neither one alone would have brought about the catastrophe, but altogether they made question and answer, problem and solution. Money was scarce. Demands were heavy. None of them except Mrs. Gregory had more than just enough. And there was this additional situation to face: there was no end of the war in sight; it gave promise now of going on indefinitely.

Joifre had said, "I nibble them." But to nibble a hole in the Germany Army might take years. They had sent Sara Lee for a few months. How about keeping her there indefinitely?

Oddly enough, it was Harvey's sister Belle who made the only protest against the recall.

"Of course, I want her back," she said slowly. "You'd understand better if you had to live with Harvey. I'm sorry, Mrs. Gregory, that he spoke to you as he did, but he's nearly crazy." She eyed the assembly with her tired shrewd eyes. "I'm no talker," she went on, "but Sara Lee has done a big thing. We don't realize, I guess, how big it is. And I think we'll just about kill her if we bring her home."

"Better to do that than to have her killed over there," some one said.

And in spite of Belle's protest, that remained the sense of the meeting. It was put to the vote and decided to recall Sara Lee. She could bring a report of conditions, and if she thought it wise an older woman could go later, to a safer place.

Belle was very quiet that evening. After dinner she went to Harvey's room and found him dressing to go out.

"I'm going with a crowd to the theater," he said. "First week of the summer stock company, you know."

He tied his tie defiantly, avoiding Belle's eyes in the mirror.

"Harvey," she said, "they're going to bring Sara Lee home."

He said nothing, but his hands shook somewhat. "And I think," Belle said, "that you will be sorry for what you have done-all the rest of your life."

XXI

By the time Henri was well enough to resume his former activities it was almost the first of May. The winter quiet was over with a vengeance, and the Allies were hammering hard with their first tolerably full supply of high-explosive shells.

Cheering reports came daily to the little house —, of rapidly augmenting armies, of big guns on caterpillar trucks that were moving slowly up to the Allied Front. Great Britain had at last learned her lesson, that only shells of immense destructiveness were of any avail against the German batteries. She was moving heaven and earth to get them, but the supply was still inadequate. With the new shells experiments were being made in barrage fire-costly experiments now and then; but the Allies were apt in learning the ugly game of modern war.

Only on the Belgian Front was there small change. The shattered army was being freshly outfitted. England was sending money and ammunition, and on the sand dunes small bodies of fresh troops drilled and smiled grimly and drilled again. But there were not, as in England and in France, great bodies of young men to draw from. Too many had been caught beyond the German wall of steel.

Yet a wave of renewed courage had come with the sun and the green fields. And conditions had improved for the Belgians in other ways. They were being paid, for one thing, with something like regularity. Food was better and more plentiful. One day Henri appeared at the top of the street and drove down triumphantly a small unclipped horse, which trundled behind it a vertical boiler on wheels with fire box and stovepipe.

"A portable kitchen!" he explained. "See, here for soup and here for coffee. And more are coming."

"Very soon, Henri, they will not need me," Sara Lee said wistfully.

But he protested almost violently. He even put the question to the horse, and blowing in his ear made him shake his head in the negative.

She was needed, indeed. To the great base hospital at La Panne went more and more wounded men. But to the little house of mercy came the small odds and ends in increasing numbers. Medical men were scarce, and badly overworked. There was talk, for a time, of sending a surgeon to the little house, but it came to nothing. La Panne was not far away, and all the surgeons they could get there were not too many.

So the little house went on much as before. Henri had moved to the mill. He was at work again, and one day, in the King's villa and quietly, because of many reasons, Henri, a very white and erect Henri, received a second medal, the highest for courage that could be given.

He did not tell Sara Lee.

But though he and the men who served under him worked hard, they could not always perform miracles. The German planes still outnumbered the Allied ones. They had grown more daring with the spring, too, and whatever Henri might learn of ground operations, he could not foretell those of the air.

On a moonlight night in early May, Sara Lee, setting out her dressings, heard a man running up the street. René challenged him sharply, only to step aside. It was Henri. He burst in on Sara Lee.

"To the cellar, mademoiselle!" he said.

"A bombardment?" asked Sara Lee.

"From the air. They may pass over, but there are twelve *taubes*, and they are circling overhead."

The first bomb dropped then in the street. It was white moonlight and the Germans must have seen that there were no troops. Probably it was as Henri said later, that they had learned of the little house, and since it brought such aid and comfort as might be it was to be destroyed.

The house of the mill went with the second bomb. Then followed a deafening uproar as plane after plane dropped its shells on the dead town. Marie and Sara Lee were in the cellar by that time, but the cellar was scarcely safer than the floor above. From a bombardment by shells from guns miles away there was protection. From a bomb dropped from the sky, the floors above were practically useless.

Only Henri and René remained on the street floor. Henri was extinguishing lights. In the passage René stood, not willing to take refuge until Henri, whom he adored, had done so. For a moment the uproar ceased, and in a spirit of bravado René stepped out into the moonlight and made a gesture of derision into the air.

He fell there, struck by a piece of splintered shell.

"Come, René!" Henri called. "The brave are those who live to fight again, not —"

But René's figure against the moonlight was gone. Henri ran to the doorway then and found him lying, his head on the little step where he had been wont to sit and whittle and sing his Tipperaree. He was dead. Henri carried him in and laid him in the little passage, very reverently. Then he went below.

"Where is René?" Sara Lee asked from the darkness.

"A foolish boy," said Henri, a catch in his throat. "He is, I think, watching these fiends of the air, from some shelter."

"There is no shelter," shivered the girl.

He groped for her hand in the darkness, and so they stood, hand in hand, like two children, waiting for what might come.

It was not until the thing was over that he told her. He had gone up first and so that she would not happen on his silent figure unwarned, had carried René to the open upper floor, where he lay, singularly peaceful, face up to the awful beauty of the night.

"Good night, little brother," Henri said to him, and left him there with a heavy heart. Never again would René sit and whittle on the doorstep and sing his tuneless Tipperaree. Never again would he gaze with boyish adoring eyes at Sara Lee as she moved back and forth in the little house.

Henri stared up at the sky. The moon looked down, cold, and cruelly bright, on the vanishing squadron of death, on the destroyed town and on the boy's white face. Somewhere, Henri felt, vanishing like the German *taubes*, but to peace instead of war, was moving René's brave and smiling spirit —a boyish angel, eager and dauntless, and still looking up.

Henri took off his cap and crossed himself.

Another sentry took René's place the next day, but the little house had lost something it could not regain. And a greater loss was to come.

Jean brought out the mail that day. For Sara Lee, moving about silent and red-eyed, there was a letter from Mr. Travers. He inclosed a hundred pounds and a clipping from a London newspaper entitled The Little House of Mercy.

"Evidently," he wrote, "you were right and we were wrong. One-half of the inclosed check is from my wife, who takes this method of showing her affectionate gratitude. The balance is from myself. Once, some months ago, I said to you that almost you restored my faith in human nature. To-day I may say that, in these hours of sorrow for us all, what you have done and are doing has brought into my gray day a breath of hope."

There was another clipping, but no comment. It recorded the death of a Reginald Alexander Travers, aged thirty.

It was then that Sara Lee, who was by way of thinking for herself those days, and of thinking clearly, recognized the strange new self-abnegation of the English-their attitude not so much of suppressing their private griefs as of refusing to obtrude them. A strongly individualistic people, they were already commencing to think nationally. Grief was a private matter, to be borne privately. To the world they must present an unbroken front, an unshaken and unshakable faith. A new attitude, and a strange one, for grumbling, crochety, gouty-souled England.

A people who had for centuries insisted not only on its rights but on its privileges was now giving as freely as ever it had demanded. It was as though, having hoarded all those years, it had but been hoarding against the day of payment. As it had received it gave-in money, in effort, in life. And without pretext.

So the Traverses, having given up all that had made life for them, sent a clipping only, and no comment. Sara Lee, through a mist of tears, saw them alone in their drawing-room, having tea as usual, and valiantly speaking of small things, and bravely facing the future, but never, in the bitterest moments, making complaint or protest.

Would America, she wondered, if her hour came, be so brave? Harvey had a phrase for such things. It was "stand the gaff." Would America stand the gaff so well? Courage was America's watchword, but a courage of the body rather than of the soul-physical courage, not moral. What would happen if America entered the struggle and the papers were filled, as were the British and the French, with long casualty lists, each name a knife thrust somewhere?

She wondered.

And then, before long, it was Sara Lee's turn to stand the gaff. There was another letter, a curiously incoherent one from Harvey's sister. She referred to something that the society had done, and hoped that Sara Lee would take it in kindness, as it was meant. Harvey was well and much happier. She was to try to understand Harvey's part. He had been almost desperate. Evidently the letter had preceded one that should have arrived at the same time. Sara Lee was sadly puzzled. She went to Henri with it, but he could make nothing out of it. There was nothing to do but to wait.

The next night Henri was to go through the lines again. Since his wounding he had been working on the Allied side, and fewer lights there were in his district that flashed the treacherous message across the flood, between night and morning. But now it was imperative that he go through the German lines again. It was feared that with grappling hooks the enemy was slowly and cautiously withdrawing the barbed wire from the inundated fields; and that could mean but one thing.

On the night he was to go Henri called Sara Lee from the crowded *salle à manger* and drawing her into the room across closed the door.

"Mademoiselle," he said gravely, "once before, long ago, you permitted me to kiss you. Will you do that for me again?"

She kissed him at once gravely. Once she would have flushed. She did not now. For there was a change in Sara Lee as well as in her outlook. She had been seeing for months the shortness of life, the brief tenure men held on it, the value of such happiness as might be for the hours that remained. She was a woman now, for all her slim young body and her charm of youth. Values had changed. To love, and to show that love, to cheer, to comfort and help-that was necessary, because soon the chance might be gone, and there would be long aching years of regret.

So she kissed him gravely and looked up into his eyes, her own full of tears.

"God bless and keep you, dear Henri," she said.

Then she went back to her work.

XXII

Much of Sara Lee's life at home had faded. She seemed to be two people. One was the girl who had knitted the afghan for Anna, and had hidden it away from Uncle James' kind but curious eyes. And one was this present Sara Lee, living on the edge of eternity, and seeing men die or suffer horribly, not to gain anything-except perhaps some honorable advancement for their souls-but that there might be preserved, at any cost, the right of honest folk to labor in their fields, to love, to pray, and at last to sleep in the peace of God.

She had lost the past and she dared not look into the future. So she was living each day as it came, with its labor, its love, its prayers and at last its sleep. Even Harvey seemed remote and stern and bitter. She reread his letters often, but they were forced. And after a time she realized another quality in them. They were self-centered. It was *his* anxiety, *his* loneliness, *his* humiliation. Sara Lee's eyes were looking out, those days, over a suffering world. Harvey's eyes were turned in on himself.

She realized this, but she never formulated it, even to herself. What she did acknowledge was a growing fear of the reunion which must come sometime-that he was cherishing still further bitterness against that day, that he would say things that he would regret later. Sometimes the thought of that day came to her when she was doing a dressing, and her hands would tremble.

Henri had not returned when, the second day after René's death, the letter came which recalled her. She opened it eagerly. Though from Harvey there usually came at the best veiled reproach, the society had always sent its enthusiastic approval.

She read it twice before she understood, and it was only when she read Belle's letter again that she began to comprehend. She was recalled; and the recall was Harvey's work.

She was very close to hating him that day. He had never understood. She would go back to him, as she had promised; but always, all the rest of their lives, there would be this barrier between them. To the barrier of his bitterness would be added her own resentment. She could never even talk to him of her work, of those great days when in her small way she had felt herself a part of the machinery of mercy of the war.

Harvey had lost something out of Sara Lee's love for him. He had done it himself, madly, despairingly. She still loved him, she felt. Nothing could change that or her promise to him. But with that love there was something now of fear. And she felt, too, that after all the years she had known him she had not known him at all. The Harvey she had known was a tender and considerate man, soft-spoken, slow to wrath, always gentle. But the Harvey of his letters and of the recall was a stranger.

It was the result of her upbringing, probably, that she had no thought of revolt. Her tie to Harvey was a real tie. By her promise to him her life was no longer hers to order. It belonged to some one else, to be ordered for her. But, though she accepted, she was too clear a thinker not to resent.

When Henri returned, toward dawn of the following night, he did not come alone. Sara Lee, rising early, found two men in her kitchen-one of them Henri, who was making coffee, and a soldier in a gray-green uniform, with a bad bruise over one eye and a sulky face. His hands were tied, but otherwise he sat at ease, and Henri, having made the coffee, held a cup to his lips.

"It is good for the spirits, man," he said in German. "Drink it."

The German took it, first gingerly, then eagerly. Henri was in high good humor.

"See, I have brought you a gift!" he exclaimed on seeing Sara Lee. "What shall we do with him? Send him to America? To show the appearance of the madmen of Europe?"

The prisoner was only a boy, such a boy as Henri himself; but a peasant, and muscular. Beside his bulk Henri looked slim as a reed. Henri eyed him with a certain tolerant humor.

"He is young, and a Bavarian," he said. "Other wise I should have killed him, for he fought hard. He has but just been called."

There was another conference in the little house that morning, but Henri's prisoner could tell little. He had heard nothing of an advance. Further along the line it was said that there was much fighting. He sat there, pale and bewildered and very civil, and in the end his frightened politeness brought about a change in the attitude of the men who questioned him. Hate all Germans as they must, who had suffered so grossly, this boy was not of those who had outraged them.

They sent him on at last, and Sara Lee was free to tell Henri her news. But she had grown very wise as to Henri's moods, and she hesitated. A certain dissatisfaction had been growing in the boy for some time, a sense of hopelessness. Further along the spring had brought renewed activity to the Allied armies. Great movements were taking place.

But his own men stood in their trenches, or what passed for trenches, or lay on their hours of relief in such wretched quarters as could be found, still with no prospect of action. No great guns, drawn by heavy tractors, came down the roads toward the trenches by the sea. Steady bombarding, incessant sniping and no movement on either side-that was the Belgian Front during the first year of the war. Inaction, with that eating anxiety as to what was going on in the occupied territory, was the portion of the heroic small army that stretched from Nieuport to Dixmude.

And Henri's nerves were not good. He was unhappy-that always-and he was not yet quite recovered from his wounds. There was on his mind, too, a certain gun which moved on a railway track, back and forth, behind the German lines, doing the work of many. He had tried to get to that gun, and failed. And he hated failure.

Certainly in this story of Sara Lee and of Henri, whose other name must not be known, allowance must be made for all those things. Yet-perhaps no allowance is enough.

Sara Lee told him that evening of her recall, told him when the shuffling of many feet in the street told of the first weary men from the trenches coming up the road.

He heard her in a dazed silence. Then:

"But you will not go?" he said. "It is impossible! You-you are needed, mademoiselle."

"What can I do, Henri? They have recalled me. My money will not come now."

"Perhaps we can arrange that. It does not cost so much. I have friends-and think, mademoiselle, how many know now of what you are doing, and love you for it. Some of them would contribute, surely."

He was desperately revolving expedients in his mind. He could himself do no more than he had done. He, or rather Jean and he together, had been bearing a full half of the expense of the little house since the beginning. But he dared not tell her that. And though he spoke hopefully, he knew well that he could raise nothing from the Belgians he knew best. Henri came of a class that held its fortunes in land, and that land was now in German hands.

"We will arrange it somehow," he said with forced cheerfulness. "No beautiful thing-and this is surely beautiful-must die because of money."

It was then that Sara Lee took the plunge.

"It is not only money, Henri."

"He has sent for you!"

Harvey was always "he" to Henri.

"Not exactly. But I think he went to some one and said I should not be here alone. You can understand how he feels. We were going to be married very soon, and then I decided to come. It made an awful upset."

Henri stood with folded arms and listened. At first he said nothing. When he spoke it was in a voice of ominous calm:

"So for a stupid convention he would destroy this beautiful thing you have made! Does he know your work? Does he know what you are to the men here? Have you ever told him?"

"I have, of course, but —"

"Do you want to go back?"

"No, Henri. Not yet. I —"

"That is enough. You are needed. You are willing to stay. I shall attend to the money. It is arranged."

"You don't understand," said Sara Lee desperately. "I am engaged to him. I can't wreck his life, can I?"

"Would it wreck your life?" he demanded. "Tell me that and I shall know how to reason with you."

But she only looked at him helplessly.

Heavy tramping in the passage told of the arrival of the first men. They did not talk and laugh as usual. As well as they could they came quietly. For René had been a good friend to many of them, and had admitted on slack nights many a weary man who had no ticket. Much as the neighbors had entered the house back home after Uncle James had gone away, came these bearded men that night. And Sara Lee, hearing their muffled voices, brushed a hand over her eyes and tried to smile.

"We can talk about it later," she said. "We mustn't quarrel. I owe so much to you, Henri."

Suddenly Henri caught her by the arm and turned her about so that she faced the lamp.

"Do you love him?" he demanded. "Sara Lee, look at me!" Only he pronounced it Saralie. "He has done a very cruel thing. Do you still love him?"

Sara Lee shut her eyes.

"I don't know. I think I do. He is very unhappy, and it is my fault."

"Your fault!"

"I must go, Henri. The men are waiting."

But he still held her arm.

"Does he love you as I love you?" he demanded. "Would he die for you?"

"That's rather silly, isn't it? Men don't die for the people they love."

"I would die for you, Saralie."

She eyed him rather helplessly.

"I don't think you mean that." Bad strategy that, for he drew her to him. His arms were like steel, and it was a rebellious and very rigid Sara Lee who found she could not free herself.

"I would die for you, Saralie!" he repeated fiercely. "That would be easier, far, than living without you. There is nothing that matters but you. Listen —I would put everything I have-my honor, my life, my hope of eternity-on one side of the scale and you on the other. And I would choose you. Is that love?" He freed her.

"It's insanity," said Sara Lee angrily. "You don't mean it. And I don't want that kind of love, if that is what you call it."

"And you will go back to that man who loves himself better than he loves you?"

"That's not true!" she flashed at him. "He is sending for me, not to get me back to him, but to get me back to safety."

"What sort of safety?" Henri demanded in an ominous tone. "Is he afraid of me?"

"He doesn't know anything about you."

"You have never told him? Why?" His eyes narrowed.

"He wouldn't have understood, Henri."

"You are going back to him," he said slowly; "and you will always keep these days of ours buried in your heart. Is that it?" His eyes softened. "I am to be a memory! Do you know what I think? I think you care for me more than you know. We have lived a lifetime together in these months. You know me better than you know him, already. We have faced death together. That is a strong tie. And I have held you in my arms. Do you think you can forget that?"

"I shall never want to forget you."

"I shall not let you forget me. You may go —I cannot prevent that perhaps. But wherever I am; Saralie, I shall stand between that lover of yours and you. And sometime I shall come from this other side of the world, and I shall find you, and you will come back with me. Back to this country-our country."

They were boyish words, but back of them was the iron determination of a man. His eyes seemed sunken in his head. His face was white. But there was almost a prophetic ring in his voice.

Sara Lee went out and left him there, went out rather terrified and bewildered, and refusing absolutely to look into her own heart.

XXIII

Late in May she started for home. It had not been necessary to close the little house. An Englishwoman of mature years and considerable wealth, hearing from Mr. Travers of Sara Lee's recall, went out a day or two before she left and took charge. She was a kindly woman, in deep mourning; and some of the ache left Sara Lee's heart when she had talked with her successor.

Perhaps, too, Mrs. Cameron understood some of the things that had puzzled her before. She had been a trifle skeptical perhaps about Sara Lee before she saw her. A young girl alone among an army of men! She was a good woman herself, and not given to harsh judgments, but the thing had seemed odd. But Sara Lee in her little house, as virginal, as without sex-consciousness as a child, Sara Lee with her shabby clothes and her stained hands and her honest eyes-this was not only a good girl, this was a brave and high-spirited and idealistic woman.

And after an evening in the house of mercy, with the soldiers openly adoring and entirely respectful, Mrs. Cameron put her arms round Sara Lee and kissed her.

"You must let me thank you," she said. "You have made me feel what I have not felt since —"

She stopped. Her mourning was only a month old. "I see to-night that, after all, many things may be gone, but that while service remains there is something worth while in life."

The next day she asked Sara Lee to stay with her, at least through the summer. Sara Lee hesitated, but at last she agreed to cable. As Henri had disappeared with the arrival of Mrs. Cameron it was that lady's chauffeur who took the message to Dunkirk and sent it off.

She had sent the cable to Harvey. It was no longer a matter of the Ladies' Aid. It was between Harvey and herself.

The reply came on the second day. It was curt and decisive.

"Now or never," was the message Harvey sent out of his black despair, across the Atlantic to the little house so close under the guns of Belgium.

Henri was half mad those last days. Jean tried to counsel him, but he was irritable, almost savage. And Jean understood. The girl had grown deep into his own heart. Like Henri, he believed that she was going back to unhappiness; he even said so to her in the car, on that last sad day when Sara Lee, having visited René's grave and prayed in the ruined church, said good-by to the little house, and went away, tearless at the last, because she was too sad for tears.

It was not for some time that Jean spoke what was in his mind, and when he had done so she turned to him gravely:

"You are wrong, Jean. He is the kindest of men. Once I am back, and safe, he will be very different. I'm afraid I've given you a wrong impression of him."

"You think then, mademoiselle, that he will forget all these months-he will never be unhappy over them?"

"Why should he?" said Sara Lee proudly. "When I tell him everything he will understand. And he will be very proud that I have done my share."

But Jean's one eye was dubious.

At the wharf in Dunkirk they found Henri, a pale but composed Henri. Jean's brows contracted. He had thought that the boy would follow his advice and stay away. But Henri was there.

It was as well, perhaps, for Sara Lee had brought him a letter, one of those missives from the trenches which had been so often left at the little house.

Henri thrust it into his pocket without reading it.

"Everything is prepared," he said. "It is the British Admiralty boat, and one of the officers has offered his cabin. You will be quite comfortable."

He appeared entirely calm. He saw to carrying Sara Lee's small bag on board; he chatted with the officers; he even wandered over to a hospital ship moored near by and exchanged civilities with a wounded man in a chair on the deck. Perhaps he swaggered a bit too much, for Jean watched him with some anxiety. He saw that the boy was taking it hard. His eyes were very sunken now, and he moved his right arm stiffly, as though the old wound troubled him.

Jean did not like leave-takings. Particularly he did not like taking leave of Sara Lee. Some time before the boat sailed he kissed her hand, and then patted it and went away in the car without looking back.

The boat was preparing to get under way. Henri was standing by her very quietly. He had not slept the night before, but then there were many nights when Henri did not sleep. He had wandered about, smoking incessantly, trying to picture the black future.

He could see no hope anywhere. America was far away, and peaceful. Very soon the tranquillity of it all would make the last months seem dreamlike and unreal. She would forget Belgium, forget him. Or she would remember him as a soldier who had once loved her. Once loved her, because she had never seemed to realize the lasting quality of his love. She had always felt that he would forget her. If he could only make her believe that he would not, it would not be so hopeless.

He had written a bit of a love letter on the little table at Dunkirk that morning, written it with the hope that the sight of the written words might carry conviction where all his protests had failed.

"I shall love you all the years of my life," he wrote. "At any time, in any place, you may come to me and know that I am waiting. Great love like this comes only once to any man, and once come to him it never goes away. At any time in the years to come you may know with certainty that you are still to me what you are now, the love of my life.

"Sometimes I think, dearest —I may call you that once, now that you have left me-that far away you will hear this call of mine and come back to me. Perhaps you will never come. Perhaps I shall not live. I feel to-day that I do not care greatly to live.

"If that is to be, then think of me somewhere, perhaps with René by my side, since he, too, loved you. And I shall still be calling you, and waiting. Perhaps even beyond the stars they have need of a little house of mercy; and, God knows, wherever I am I shall have need of you."

He had the letter in the pocket of his tunic, and at last the moment came when the boat must leave. Suddenly Henri knew that he could not allow her to cross to England alone. The last few days had brought many stories of submarine attacks. Here, so far north, the Germans were particularly active. They had for a long time lurked in waiting for this British Admiralty boat, with its valuable cargo, its officers and the government officials who used it.

"Good-by, Henri," said Sara Lee. "I —of course it is no use to try to tell you —"

"I am going across with you."

"But —"

"I allowed you to come over alone. I shiver when I think of it. I shall take you back myself."

"Is it very dangerous?"

"Probably not. But can you think of me standing safe on that quay and letting you go into danger alone?"

"I am not afraid."

"I know that. I have never seen you afraid. But if you wish to see a coward, look at me. I am a coward for you."

He put his hand into his pocket. It occurred to him to give her the letter now so that if anything happened she would at least have had it. He wanted no mistake about that appointment beyond the stars. But the great world of eternity was very large, and they must have a definite understanding about that meeting at the little house of mercy Over There.

Perhaps he had a little fever that day. He was alternately flushed and pale; and certainly he was not quite rational. His hand shook as he brought out her letter-and with it the other letter, from the Front.

"Have you the time to come with me?" Sara Lee asked doubtfully. "I want you to come, of course, but if your work will suffer —"

He held out his letter to her.

"I shall go away," he said, "while you read it. And perhaps you will not destroy it, because —I should like to feel that you have it always."

He went away at once, saluting as he passed other officers, who gravely saluted him. On the deck of the hospital ship the invalid touched his cap. Word was going about, in the stealthy manner of such things, that Henri whose family name we may not know, was a brave man and doing brave things.

The steamer had not yet cast off. As usual, it was to take a flying start from the harbor, for it was just outside the harbor that the wolves of the sea lay in wait. Henri, alone at last, opened his letter, and stood staring at it. There was again movement behind the German line, a matter to be looked into, as only he could do it. Probably nothing, as before; but who could say?

Henri looked along the shore to where but a few miles away lay the ragged remnant of his country. And he looked forward to where Sara Lee, his letter in her hand, was staring blindly at nothing. Then he looked out toward the sea, where lay who knew what dangers of death and suffering.

After that first moment of indecision he never hesitated. He stood on the deck and watched, rather frozen and rigid, and with a mind that had ceased working, while the steamer warped out from the quay. If in his subconsciousness there was any thought it was doubtless that he had done his best for a long time, and that he had earned the right to protect for a few hours the girl he loved. That, too, there had been activity along the German-Belgian line before, without result.

Perhaps subconsciously those things were there. He himself was conscious of no thought, of only a dogged determination to get Sara Lee across the channel safely. He put everything else behind him. He counted no cost.

The little admiralty boat sped on. In the bow, on the bridge, and at different stations lookouts kept watch. The lifeboats were hung overboard, ready to lower instantly. On the horizon a British destroyer steamed leisurely. Henri stood for a long time on the deck. The land fell away quickly. From a clear silhouette of the town against the sky-the dunes, the spire of the cathedral, the roof of the *mairie* —it became vague, shadowy-the height of a hand —a line-nothing.

Henri roused himself. He was very thirsty, and the wound in his arm ached. When he raised his hand to salute the movement was painful.

It was a very grave Sara Lee he found in the officer's cabin when he went inside later on. She was sitting on the long seat below the open port, her hat slightly askew and her hands folded in her lap. Her bag was beside her, and there was in her eyes a perplexity Henri was too wretched to notice.

For the first time Sara Lee was realizing the full value of the thing she was throwing away. She had persistently discounted it until now. She had been grateful for it. She had felt unworthy of it. But now, on the edge of leaving it, she felt that something infinitely precious and very beautiful was going out of her life. She had already a sense of loss.

For the first time, too, she was allowing herself to think of certain contingencies that were now forever impossible. For instance, suppose she had stayed with Mrs. Cameron? Suppose she had broken her promise to Harvey and remained at the little house? Suppose she had done as Henri had so wildly urged her, and had broken entirely with Harvey? Would she have married Henri?

There was a certain element of caution in the girl. It made the chances she had taken rather more courageous, indeed, because she had always counted the cost. But marriage was not a matter for taking chances. One should know not only the man, but his setting, though she would not have thought of it in that way. Not only the man, but the things that made up his life-his people, his home.

And Henri was to her still a figure, not so much now of mystery as of detachment. Except Jean he had no intimates. He had no family on the only side of the line she knew. He had not even a country.

She had reached that point when Henri came below and saluted her stiffly from the doorway.

"Henri!" she said. "I believe you are ill!"

"I am not ill," he said, and threw himself into the corner of the seat. "You have read it?"

She nodded. Even thinking of it brought a lump into her throat. He bent forward, but he did not touch her.

"I meant it, Saralie," he said. "Sometimes men are infatuated, and write what they do not mean. They are sincere at the time, and then later on-But I meant it. I shall always mean it."

Not then, nor during the three days in London, did he so much as take her hand. He was not well. He ate nothing, and at night he lay awake and drank a great deal of water. Once or twice he found her looking at him anxiously, but he disclaimed all illness.

He had known from the beginning what he was doing. But he did not touch her, because in his heart he knew that where once he had been worthy he was no longer worthy. He had left his work for a woman.

It is true that he had expected to go back at once. But the *Philadelphia*, which had been listed to sail the next day, was held up by a strike in Liverpool, and he waited on, taking such hours as she could give him, feverishly anxious to make her happy, buying her little gifts, mostly flowers, which she wore tucked in her belt and smiled over, because she had never before received flowers from a man.

He was alternately gay and silent. They walked across the Thames by the Parliament buildings, and midway across he stopped and looked long at the stream. And they went to the Zoölogical Gardens, where he gravely named one of the sea lions for Colonel Lilias because of its mustache, and insisted on saluting it each time before he flung it a fish. Once he soberly gathered up a very new baby camel, all legs, in his arms, and presented it to her.

"Please accept it, mademoiselle," he said. "With my compliments."

They dined together every night, very modestly, sitting in some crowded restaurant perhaps, but seeing little but each other. Sara Lee had bought a new hat in London-black, of course, but faced with white. He adored her in it. He would sit for long moments, his elbows propped on the table, his blond hair gleaming in the candlelight, and watch her.

"I wonder," he said once, "if you had never met him would you have loved me?"

"I do love you, Henri."

"I don't want that sort of love." And he had turned his head away.

But one evening he called for her at Morley's, a white and crushed boy, needing all that she could give him and much more. He came as a man goes to the woman he loves when he is in trouble, much as a child to his mother. Sara Lee, coming down to the reception room, found him alone there, walking rapidly up and down. He turned desperate eyes on her.

"I have brought bad news," he said abruptly.

"The little house —"

"I do not know. I ran away, mademoiselle. I am a traitor. And the Germans broke through last night."

"Henri!"

"They broke through. We were not ready. That is what I have done."

"Don't you think," Sara Lee said in a frozen voice, "that is what I have done? I let you come."

"You? You are taking the blame? Mademoiselle, I have enough to bear without that."

He explained further, still standing in his rigid attitude. If he had been white before at times he was ghastly now. It had not been an attack in force. A small number had got across and had penetrated beyond the railway line. There had been hand-to-hand fighting in the road beyond the poplars. But it looked more like an experiment, an endeavor to discover the possibility of a real advance through the inundation; or perhaps a feint to cover operations elsewhere.

"For every life lost I am responsible," he ended in a flat and lifeless tone.

"But you might not have known," she protested wildly. "Even if you had been there, Henri, you might not have known." She knew something of war by that time. "How could you have told that a small movement of troops was to take place?"

"I should have been there."

"But-if they came without warning?"

"I did not tell you," he said, looking away from her. "There had been a warning. I disregarded it."

He went back to Belgium that night. Sara Lee, at the last, held out her hand. She was terrified for him, and she showed it.

"I shall not touch your hand," he said. "I have forfeited my right to do that." Then, seeing what was in her face, he reassured her. "I shall not do *that*," he said. "It would be easier. But I shall have to go back and see what can be done."

He was the old Henri to the last, however. He went carefully over her steamship ticket, and inquired with equal care into the amount of money she had.

"It will take you home?" he asked.

"Very comfortably, Henri."

"It seems very little."

Then he said, apropos of nothing: "Poor Jean!"

When he left her at last he went to the door, very erect and soldierly. But he turned there and stood for a moment looking at her, as though through all that was coming he must have with him, to give him strength, that final picture of her.

The elderly chambermaid, coming into Sara Lee's room the next morning, found her fully dressed in the frock she had worn the night before, face down on her bed.

XXIV

It was early in June when at last the lights went down behind the back drop and came up in front, to show Sara Lee knitting again, though not by the fire. The amazing interlude was over.

Over, except in Sara Lee's heart. The voyage had been a nightmare. She had been ill for one thing—a combination of seasickness and heartsickness. She had allowed Henri to come to England with her, and the Germans had broken through. All the good she had done-and she had helped-was nothing to this mischief she had wrought.

It had been a small raid. She gathered that from the papers on board. But that was not the vital thing. What mattered was that she had let a man forget his duty to his country in his solicitude for her.

But as the days went on the excitement of her return dulled the edge of her misery somewhat. The thing was done. She could do only one thing to help. She would never go back, never again bring trouble and suffering where she had meant only to bring aid and comfort.

She had a faint hope that Harvey would meet her at the pier. She needed comforting and soothing, and perhaps a bit of praise. She was so very tired; depressed, too, if the truth be known. She needed a hand to lead her back to her old place on the stage, and kind faces to make her forget that she had ever gone away.

Because that was what she had to do. She must forget Henri and the little house on the road to the poplar trees; and most of all, she must forget that because of her Henri had let the Germans through.

But Harvey did not meet her. There was a telegram saying he would meet her train if she wired when she was leaving-an exultant message breathing forgiveness and signed "with much love." She flushed when she read it.

Of course he could not meet her in New York. This was not the Continent in wartime, where convention had died of a great necessity. And he was not angry, after all. A great wave of relief swept over her. But it was odd how helpless she felt. Since her arrival in England months before there had always been Henri to look after things for her. It was incredible to recall how little she had done for herself.

Was she glad to be back? She did not ask herself. It was as though the voyage had automatically detached her from that other Sara Lee of the little house. That was behind her, a dream —a mirage-or a memory. Here, a trifle confused by the bustle, was once again the Sara Lee who had knitted for Anna, and tended the plants in the dining-room window, and watched Uncle James slowly lowered into his quiet grave.

Part of her detachment was voluntary. She could not bear to remember.

She had but to close her eyes to see Henri's tragic face that last night at Morley's. And part of the detachment was because, after all, the interlude had been but a matter of months, and reaching out familiar hands to her were the habits and customs and surroundings of all the earlier years of her life, drawing her back to them.

It was strange how Henri's face haunted her. She could close her eyes and see it, line by line, his very swagger-for he did swagger, just a little; his tall figure and unruly hair; his long, narrow, muscular hands. Strange and rather uncomfortable. Because she could not summon Harvey's image at all. She tried to bring before her, that night in the train speeding west, his solid figure and kind eyes as they would greet her the next day-tried, and failed. All she got was the profile of the photograph, and the stubborn angle of the jaw.

She was up very early the next morning, and it was then, as the train rolled through familiar country, that she began to find Harvey again. A flush of tenderness warmed her. She must be very kind to him because of all that he had suffered.

The train came to a stop. Rather breathless Sara Lee went out on the platform. Harvey was there, in the crowd. He did not see her at first. He was looking toward the front of the train. So her first glimpse of him was the view of the photograph. His hat was off, and his hair, carefully brushed back, gave him the eager look of the picture.

He was a strong and manly figure, as unlike Henri as an oak is unlike one of Henri's own tall and swaying poplars. Sara Lee drew a long breath. Here after all were rest and peace; love and gentleness; quiet days and still evenings. No more crowds and wounds and weary men, no more great thunderings of guns, no imminence of death. Rest and peace.

Then Harvey saw her, and the gleam of happiness and relief in his eyes made her own eyes misty. She saw even in that first glance that he looked thinner and older. A pang of remorse shot through her. Was happiness always bought at the cost of happiness? Did one always take away in order to give? Not in so many words, but in a flash of doubt the thought went through her mind.

There was no reserve in Harvey's embrace. He put his arms about her and held her close. He did not speak at first. Then:

"My own little girl," he said. "My own little girl!"

Suddenly Sara Lee was very happy. All her doubts were swept away by his voice, his arms. There was no thrill for her in his caress, but there were peace and quiet joy. It was enough for her, just then, that she had brought back some of the happiness she had robbed him of.

"Oh, Harvey!" she said. "I'm glad to be back again-with you."

He held her off then and looked at her.

"You are thin," he said. "You're not pale, but you are thin." And in a harder voice: "What did they do to you over there?"

But he did not wait for a reply. He did not seem to want one. He picked up her bag, and guiding her by the elbow, piloted her through the crowd.

"A lot of folks wanted to come and meet you," he said, "but I steered them off. You'd have thought Roosevelt was coming to town the way they've been calling up."

"To meet me?"

"I expect the Ladies' Aid Society wanted to get into the papers again," he said rather grimly. "They are merry little advertisers, all right."

"I don't think that, Harvey."

"Well, I do," he said, and brought her to a stop facing a smart little car, very new, very gay. "How do you like it?" he asked.

"Like it? Why, it's not yours, is it?"

"Surest thing you know. Or, rather, it's ours. Had a few war babies, and they grew up."

Sara Lee looked at it, and for just an instant, a rather sickening instant, she saw Henri's shattered low car, battle-scarred and broken.

"It's —lovely," said Sara Lee. And Harvey found no fault with her tone.

Sara Lee had intended to go to Anna's, for a time at least. But she found that Belle was expecting her and would not take no.

"She's moved the baby in with the others," Harvey explained as he took the wheel. "Wait until you see your room. I knew we'd be buying furniture soon, so I fixed it up."

He said nothing for a time. He was new to driving a car, and the traffic engrossed him. But when they had reached a quieter neighborhood he put a hand over hers.

"Good God, how I've been hungry for you!" he said. "I guess I was pretty nearly crazy sometimes." He glanced at her apprehensively, but if she knew his connection with her recall she showed no resentment. As a matter of fact there was in his voice something that reminded her of Henri, the same deeper note, almost husky.

She was, indeed, asking herself very earnestly what was there in her of all people that should make two men care for her as both Henri and Harvey cared. In the humility of all modest women she was bewildered. It made her rather silent and a little sad. She was so far from being what they thought her.

Harvey, stealing a moment from the car to glance at her, saw something baffling in her face.

"Do you still care, Sara Lee?" he asked almost diffidently. "As much as ever?"

"I have come back to you," she said after an imperceptible pause.

"Well, I guess that's the answer."

He drew a deep satisfied breath. "I used to think of you over there, and all those foreigners in uniform strutting about, and it almost got me, some times."

And again, as long before, he read into her passivity his own passion, and was deeply content.

Belle was waiting on the small front porch. There was an anxious frown on her face, and she looked first, not at Sara Lee, but at Harvey. What she saw there evidently satisfied her, for the frown disappeared. She kissed Sara Lee impulsively.

All that afternoon, much to Harvey's resentment, Sara Lee received callers. The Ladies' Aid came en masse and went out to the dining-room and there had tea and cake. Harvey disappeared when they came.

"You are back," he said, "and safe, and all that. But it's not their fault. And I'll be hanged if I'll stand round and listen to them."

He got his hat and then, finding her alone in a back hall for a moment, reverted uneasily to the subject.

"There are two sides to every story," he said. "They're going to knife me this afternoon, all right. Damned hypocrites! You just keep your head, and I'll tell you my side of it later."

"Harvey," she said slowly, "I want to know now just what you did. I'm not angry. I've never been angry. But I ought to know."

It was a very one-sided story that Harvey told her, standing in the little back hall, with Belle's children hanging over the staircase and begging for cake. Yet in the main it was true. He had reached his limit of endurance. She was in danger, as the photograph plainly showed. And a fellow had a right to fight for his own happiness.

"I wanted you back, that's all," he ended. And added an anticlimax by passing a plate of sliced jelly roll through the stair rail to the clamoring children.

Sara Lee stood there for a moment after he had gone. He was right, or at least he had been within his rights. She had never even heard of the new doctrine of liberty for women. There was nothing in her training to teach her revolt. She was engaged to Harvey; already, potentially, she belonged to him. He had interfered with her life, but he had had the right to interfere.

And also there was in the back of her mind a feeling that was almost guilt. She had let Henri tell her he loved her. She had even kissed him. And there had been many times in the little house when Harvey, for days at a time, had not even entered her thoughts. There was, therefore, a very real tenderness in the face she lifted for his good-by kiss.

To Belle in the front hall Harvey gave a firm order.

"Don't let any reporters in," he said warningly. "This is strictly our affair. It's a private matter. It's nobody's business what she did over there. She's home. That's all that matters."

Belle assented, but she was uneasy. She knew that Harvey was unreasonably, madly jealous of Sara Lee's work at the little house of mercy, and she knew him well enough to know that sooner or later he would show that jealousy. She felt, too, that the girl should have been allowed her small triumph without interference. There had been interference enough already. But it was easier to yield to Harvey than to argue with him.

It was rather a worried Belle who served tea that afternoon in her dining room, with Mrs. Gregory pouring; the more uneasy, because already she divined a change in Sara Lee. She was as lovely as ever, even lovelier. But she had a poise, a steadiness, that were new; and silences in which, to Belle's shrewd eyes, she seemed to be weighing things.

Reporters clamored to see Sara Lee that day, and, failing to see her, telephoned Harvey at his office to ask if it was true that she had been decorated by the King. He was short to the point of affront.

"I haven't heard anything about it," he snapped. "And I wouldn't say if I had. But it's not likely. What d'you fellows think she was doing anyhow? Leading a charge? She was running a soup kitchen. That's all."

He hung up the receiver with a jerk, but shortly after that he fell to pacing his small office. She had not said anything about being decorated, but the reporters had said it had been in a London newspaper. If she had not told him that, there were probably many things she had not told him. But of course there had been very little time. He would see if she mentioned it that night.

Sara Lee had had a hard day. The children loved her. In the intervals of calls they crawled over her, and the littlest one called her Saralie. She held the child in her arms close.

"Saralie!" said the child, over and over; "Saralie! That's your name. I love your name."

And there came, echoing in her ears, Henri and his tender Saralie.

There was an oppression on her too. Her very bedroom thrust on her her approaching marriage. This was her own furniture, for her new home. It was beautiful, simple and good. But she was not ready for marriage. She had been too close to the great struggle to be prepared to think in terms of peace so soon. Perhaps, had she dared to look deeper than that, she would have found something else, a something she had not counted on.

She and Belle had a little time after the visitors had gone, before Harvey came home. They sat in Belle's bedroom, and her sentences were punctuated by little backs briskly presented to have small garments fastened, or bows put on stiffly bobbed yellow hair.

"Did you understand my letter?" she asked. "I was sorry I had sent it, but it was too late then."

"I put your letter and-theirs, together. I supposed that Harvey —"

"He was about out of his mind," Belle said in her worried voice. "Stand still, Mary Ellen! He went to Mrs. Gregory, and I suppose he said a good bit. You know the way he does. Anyhow, she was very angry. She called a special meeting, and —I tried to prevent their recalling you. He doesn't know that, of course."

"You tried?"

"Well, I felt as though it was your work," Belle said rather uncomfortably. "Bring me the comb, Alice. I guess we get pretty narrow here and —I've been following things more closely since you went over. I know more than I did. And, of course, after one marries there isn't much chance. There are children and —" Her face twisted. "I wish I could do something."

She got up and brought from the dresser a newspaper clipping.

"It's the London newspaper," she explained. "I've been taking it, but Harvey doesn't know. He doesn't care much for the English. This is about your being decorated."

Sara Lee held it listlessly in her hands.

"Shall I tell him, Belle?" she asked.

Belle hesitated.

"I don't believe I would," she said forlornly. "He won't like it. That's why I've never showed him that clipping. He hates it all so."

Sara Lee dressed that evening in the white frock. She dressed slowly, thinking hard. All round her was the shiny newness of her furniture, a trifle crowded in Belle's small room. Sara Lee had a terrible feeling of being fastened in by it. Wherever she turned it gleamed. She felt surrounded, smothered.

She had meant to make a clean breast of things-of the little house, and of Henri, and of the King, pinning the medal on her shabby black jacket and shaking hands with her. Henri she must tell about-not his name of course, nor his madness, nor even his love. But she felt that she owed it to Harvey to have as few secrets from him as possible. She would tell about what the boy had done for her, and how he, and he alone, had made it all possible.

Surely Harvey would understand. It was a page that was closed. It had held nothing to hurt him. She had come back.

She stood by her window, thinking. And a breath of wind set the leaves outside to rustling. Instantly she was back again in the little house, and the sound was not leaves, but the shuffling of many stealthy feet on the cobbles of the street at night, that shuffling that was so like the rustling of leaves in a wood or the murmur of water running over a stony creek bed.

XXV

It was clear to Sara Lee from the beginning of the evening that Harvey did not intend to hear her story. He did not say so; indeed, for a time he did not talk at all. He sat with his arms round her, content just to have her there.

"I have a lot of arrears to make up," he said. "I've got to get used to having you where I can touch you. To-night when I go upstairs I'm going to take that damned colorless photograph of you and throw it out the window."

"I must tell you about your photograph," she ventured. "It always stood on the mantel over the stove, and when there was a threatened bombardment I used to put it under —"

"Let's not talk, honey."

When he came out of that particular silence he said abruptly:

"Will Leete is dead."

"Oh, no! Poor Will Leete."

"Died of pneumonia in some God-forsaken hole over there. He's left a wife and nothing much to keep her. That's what comes of mixing in the other fellow's fight. I guess we can get the house as soon as we want it. She has to sell; and it ought to be a bargain."

"Harvey," she said rather timidly, "you speak of the other fellow's fight. They say over there that we are sure to be drawn into it sooner or later."

"Not on our life!" he replied brusquely. "And if you don't mind, honey, I don't care to hear about what they think over there." He got up from his old place on the arm of her chair and stood on the rug. "I'd better tell you now how I feel about this thing. I can't talk about it, that's all. We'll finish up now and let it go at that. I'm sorry there's a war. I'll send money when I can afford it, to help the Belgians, though my personal opinion is that they're getting theirs for what they did in the Congo. But I don't want to hear about what you did over there."

He saw her face, and he went to her and kissed her cheek.

"I don't want to hurt you, honey," he said. "I love you with all my heart. But somehow I can't forget that you left me and went over there when there was no reason for it. You put off our marriage, and I suppose we'd better get it over. Go ahead and tell me about it."

He drew up a chair and waited, but the girl smiled rather tremulously.

"Perhaps we'd better wait, if you feel that way, Harvey."

His face was set as he looked at her.

"There's only one thing I want to know," he said. "And I've got a right to know that. You're a young girl, and you're beautiful-to me, anyhow. You've been over there with a lot of crazy foreigners." He got up again and all the bitterness of the empty months was in his voice. "Did any of them-was there anybody there you cared about?"

"I came back, Harvey."

"That's not the question."

"There were many men-officers-who were kind to me. I —"

"That's not the question, either."

"If I had loved any one more than I loved you I should not have come back."

"Wait a minute!" he said quickly. "You had to come back, you know."

"I could have stayed. The Englishwoman who took over my work asked me to stay on and help her."

He was satisfied then. He went back to the arm of her chair and kissed her.

"All right," he said. "I've suffered the tortures of the damned, but-that fixes it. Now let's talk about something else. I'm sick of this war talk."

"I'd like to tell you about my little house. And poor René —"

"Who was René?" he demanded.

"The orderly."

"The one on the step, with a rifle?"

"Yes."

"Look here," he said. "I've got to get to all that gradually. I don't know that I'll ever get to it cheerfully. But I can't talk about that place to-night. And I don't want to talk war. The whole business makes me sick. I've got a car out of it, and if things keep on we may be able to get the Leete house. But there's no reason in it, no sense. I'm sick to death of hearing about it. Let's talk of something else."

But-and here was something strange-Sara Lee could find nothing else to talk about. The thing that she had looked forward so eagerly to telling-that was barred. And the small gossip of their little circle, purely personal and trivial, held only faint interest for her. For the first time they had no common ground to meet on.

Yet it was a very happy man who went whistling to his room that night. He was rather proud of himself too. After all the bitterness of the past months, he had been gentle and loving to Sara Lee. He had not scolded her.

In the next room he could hear her going quietly about, opening and closing the drawers of the new bureau, moving a chair. Pretty soon, God willing, they need never be separated. He would have her always, to protect and cherish and love.

He went outside to her closed door.

"Good night, sweetheart," he called softly.

"Good night, dear," came her soft reply.

But long after he was asleep Sara Lee stood at her window and listened to the leaves, so like the feet of weary men on the ruined street over there.

For the first time she was questioning the thing she had done. She loved Harvey-but there were many kinds of love. There was the love of Jean for Henri, and there was the wonderful love, though the memory now was cruel and hurt her, of Henri for herself. And there was the love of Marie for the memory of Maurice the spy. Many kinds of love; and one heart might love many people, in different ways.

A small doubt crept into her mind. This feeling she had for Harvey was not what she had thought it was over there. It was a thing that had belonged to a certain phase of her life. But that phase was over. It was, like Marie's, but a memory.

This Harvey of the new car and the increased income and the occasional hardness in his voice was not the Harvey she had left. Or perhaps it was she who had changed. She wondered. She felt precisely the same, tender toward her friends, unwilling to hurt them. She did not want to hurt Harvey.

But she did not love him as he deserved to be loved. And she had a momentary lift of the veil, when she saw the long vista of the years, the two of them always together and always between them hidden, untouched, but eating like a cancer, Harvey's resentment and suspicion of her months away from him.

There would always be a barrier between them. Not only on Harvey's side. There were things she had no right to tell-of Henri, of his love and care for her, and of that last terrible day when he realized what he had done.

That night, lying in the new bed, she faced that situation too. How much was she to blame? If Henri felt that each life lost was lost by him wasn't the same true for her? Why had she allowed him to stay in London?

But that was one question she did not answer frankly.

She lay there in the darkness and wondered what punishment he would receive. He had done so much for them over there. Surely, surely, they would allow for that. But small things came back to her-the awful sight of the miller and his son, led away to death, with the sacks over their heads. The relentlessness of it all, the expecting that men should give everything, even life itself, and ask for no mercy.

And this, too, she remembered: Once in a wild moment Henri had said he would follow her to America, and that there he would prove to her that his and not Harvey's was the real love of her life-the great love, that comes but once to any woman, and to some not at all. Yet on that last night at Morley's he had said what she now felt was a final farewell. That last look of his, from the doorway-that had been the look of a man who would fill his eyes for the last time.

She got up and stood by the window. What had they done to him? What would they do? She looked at her watch. It was four o'clock in the morning over there. The little house would be quiet now, but down along the lines men would be standing on the firing step of the trench, and waiting, against what the dawn might bring.

Through the thin wall came the sound of Harvey's heavy, regular breathing. She remembered Henri's light sleeping on the kitchen floor, his cap on the table, his cape rolled round him —a sleeping, for all his weariness, so light that he seemed always half conscious. She remembered the innumerable times he had come in at this hour, muddy, sometimes rather gray of face with fatigue, but always cheerful.

It was just such an hour that she found him giving hot coffee to the German prisoner. It had been but a little earlier when he had taken her to the roof and had there shown her René, lying with his face up toward the sky which had sent him death.

A hundred memories crowded-Henri's love for the Belgian soldiers, and theirs for him; his humor; his absurd riddles. There was the one he had asked René, the very day before the air attack. He had stood stiffly and frowningly before the boy, and he had asked in a highly official tone:

"What must a man be to be buried with military honors?"

"A general?"

"No."

"An officer?"

"No, no! Use your head boy! This is very important. A mistake would be most serious."

René had shaken his head dejectedly.

"He must be dead, René," Henri had said gravely. "Entirely dead. As I said, it is well to know these things. A mistake would be unfortunate."

His blue eyes had gleamed with fun, but his face had remained frowning. It was quite five minutes before she had heard René chuckling on the doorstep.

Was he still living, this Henri of the love of life and courting of death? Could anything so living die? And if he had died had it been because of her? She faced that squarely for the first time.

"Perhaps even beyond the stars they have need of a little house of mercy; and, God knows, wherever I am I shall have need of you."

Beyond the partition Harvey slept on, his arms under his head.

XXVI

Harvey was clamoring for an early wedding. And indeed there were few arguments against it, save one that Sara Lee buried in her heart. Belle's house was small, and though she was welcome there, and more than that, Sara Lee knew that she was crowding the family.

Perhaps Sara Lee would have agreed in the end. There seemed to be nothing else to do, though by the end of the first week she was no longer in any doubt as to what her feeling for Harvey really was. It was kindness, affection; but it was not love. She would marry him because she had promised to, and because their small world expected her to do so; and because she could not shame him again.

For to her surprise she found that that was what he had felt —a strange, self-conscious shame, like that of a man who has been jilted. She felt that by coming back to him she had forfeited the right to break the engagement.

So every hour of every day seemed to make the thing more inevitable. Belle was embroidering towels for her in her scant leisure. Even Anna, with a second child coming, sent in her contribution to the bride's linen chest. By almost desperately insisting on a visit to Aunt Harriet she got a reprieve of a month. And Harvey was inclined to be jealous even of that.

Sometimes, but mostly at night when she was alone, a hot wave of resentment overwhelmed her. Why should she be forced into the thing? Was there any prospect of happiness after marriage when there was so little before?

For she realized now that even Harvey was not happy. He had at last definitely refused to hear the story of the little house.

"I'd rather just forget it, honey!" he said.

But inconsistently he knew she did not forget it, and it angered him. True to his insistence on ignoring those months of her absence, she made no attempt to tell him. Now and then, however, closed in the library together, they would fail of things to talk about, and Sara Lee's knitting needles would be the only sound in the room. At those times he would sit back in his chair and watch the far-away look in her eyes, and it maddened him.

From her busy life Belle studied them both, with an understanding she did not reveal. And one morning when the mail came she saw Sara Lee's face as she turned away, finding there was no letter for her, and made an excuse to follow her to her room.

The girl was standing by the window looking out. The children were playing below, and the maple trees were silent. Belle joined her there and slipped an arm round her.

"Why are you doing it, Sara Lee?" she asked.

"Doing what?"

"Marrying Harvey."

Sara Lee looked at her with startled eyes.

"I'm engaged to him, Belle. I've promised."

"Exactly," said Belle dryly. "But that's hardly a good reason, is it? It takes more than a promise." She stared down at the flock of children in the yard below. "Harvey's a man," she said. "He doesn't understand, but I do. You've got to care a whole lot, Sara Lee, if you're going to go through with it. It takes a lot of love, when it comes to having children and all that."

"He's so good, Belle. How can I hurt him?"

"You'll hurt him a lot more by marrying him when you don't love him."

"If only I could have a little time," she cried wildly. "I'm so —I'm tired, Belle. And I can't forget about the war and all that. I've tried. Sometimes I think if we could talk it over together I'd get it out of my mind."

"He won't talk about it?"

"He's my own brother, and I love him dearly. But sometimes I think he's hard. Not that he's ever ugly," she hastened to add; "but he's stubborn. There's a sort of wall in him, and he puts some things behind it. And it's like beating against a rock to try to get at them."

After a little silence she said hesitatingly:

"We've got him to think of too. He has a right to be happy. Sometimes I've looked at you—you're so pretty, Sara Lee-and I've wondered if there wasn't some one over there who-cared for you."

"There was one man, an officer-Oh, Belle, I can't tell you. Not *you!*"

"Why not!" asked Belle practically. "You ought to talk it out to some one, and if Harvey insists on being a fool that's his own fault."

For all the remainder of that sunny morning Sara Lee talked what was in her heart. And Belle-poor, romantic, starved Belle-heard and thrilled. She made buttonholes as she listened, but once or twice a new tone in Sara Lee's voice caused her to look up. Here was a new Sara Lee, a creature of vibrant voice and glowing eyes; and Belle was not stupid. She saw that it was Henri whose name brought the deeper note.

Sara Lee had stopped with her recall, had stopped and looked about the room with its shiny new furniture and had shivered. Belle bent over her work.

"Why don't you go back?" she asked.

Sara Lee looked at her piteously.

"How can I? There is Harvey. And the society would not send me again. It's over, Belle. All over."

After a pause Belle said: "What's become of Henri? He hasn't written, has he?"

Sara Lee got up and went to the window.

"I don't know where he is. He may be dead."

Her voice was flat and lifeless. Belle knew all that she wanted to know. She rose and gathered up her sewing.

"I'm going to talk to Harvey. You're not going to be rushed into a wedding. You're tired, and it's all nonsense. Well, I'll have to run now and dress the children."

That night Harvey and Belle had almost a violent scene. He had taken Sara Lee over the Leete house that evening. Will Leete's widow had met them there, a small sad figure in her mourning, but very composed, until she opened the door into a tiny room upstairs with a desk and a lamp in it.

"This was Will's study," she said. "He did his work here in the evenings, and I sat in that little chair and sewed. I never thought then —" Her lips quivered.

"Pretty rotten of Will Leete to leave that little thing alone," said Harvey on their way home. "He had his fling; and she's paying for it."

But Sara Lee was silent. It was useless to try to make Harvey understand the urge that had called Will Leete across the sea to do his share for the war, and that had brought him that peace of God that passeth all understanding.

It was not a good time for Belle to put up to him her suggestion for a delay in the marriage, that evening after their return. He took it badly and insisted on sending upstairs for Sara Lee.

"Did you ask Belle to do this?" he demanded bluntly.

"To do what?"

"To put things off."

"I have already told you, Harvey," Belle put in. "It is my own idea. She is tired. She's been through a lot. I've heard the story you're too stubborn to listen to. And I strongly advise her to wait a while."

And after a time he agreed ungraciously. He would buy the house and fix it over, and in the early fall it would be ready.

"Unless," he added to Sara Lee with a bitterness born of disappointment —"unless you change your mind again."

He did not kiss her that night when she and Belle went together up the stairs. But he stared after her gloomily, with hurt and bewilderment in his eyes.

He did not understand. He never would. She had come home to him all gentleness and tenderness, ready to find in him the things she needed so badly. But out of his obstinacy and hurt he had himself built up a barrier.

That night Sara Lee dreamed that she was back in the little house of mercy. René was there; and Henri; and Jean, with the patch over his eye. They were waiting for the men to come, and the narrow hall was full of the odor of Marie's soup. Then she heard them coming, the shuffling of many feet on the road. She went to the door, with Henri beside her, and watched them coming up the road, a deeper shadow in the blackness-tired men, wounded men, homeless men coming to her little house with its firelight and its warmth. Here and there the match that lighted a cigarette showed a white but smiling face. They stopped before the door, and the warm little house, with its guarded lights and its food and cheer, took them in.

XXVII

Very pale and desperate, Henri took the night A train for Folkestone after he had said good-by to Sara Lee. He alternately chilled and burned with fever, and when he slept, as he did now and then, going off suddenly into a doze and waking with a jerk, it was to dream of horrors.

He thought, in his wilder intervals, of killing himself. But his code did not include such a shirker's refuge. He was going back to tell his story and to take his punishment.

He had cabled to Jean to meet him at Calais, but when, at dawn the next morning, the channel boat drew in to the wharf there was no sign of Jean or the car. Henri regarded the empty quay with apathetic eyes. They would come, later on. If he could only get his head down and sleep for a while he would be better able to get toward the Front. For he knew now that he was ill. He had, indeed, been ill for days, but he did not realize that. And he hated illness. He regarded it with suspicion, as a weakness not for a strong man.

The drowsy girl in her chair at the Gare Maritime regarded him curiously and with interest. Many women turned to look after Henri, but he did not know this. Had he known it he would have regarded it much as he did illness.

The stupid boy was not round. The girl herself took the key and led the way down the long corridor upstairs to a room. Henri stumbled in and fell across the bed. He was almost immediately asleep.

Late in the afternoon he wakened. Strange that Jean had not come. He got up and bathed his face. His right arm was very stiff now, and pains ran from the old wound in his chest down to the fingers of his hand. He tried to exercise to limber it, and grew almost weak with pain.

At six o'clock, when Jean had not come, Henri resorted to ways that he knew of and secured a car. He had had some coffee by that time, and he felt much better-so well indeed that he sang under his breath a strange rambling song that sounded rather like René's rendering of Tipperary. The driver looked at him curiously every now and then.

It was ten o'clock when they reached La Panne. Henri went at once to the villa set high on a sand dune where the King's secretary lived. The house was dark, but in the library at the rear there was a light. He stumbled along the paths beside the house, and reached at last, after interminable miles, when the path sometimes came up almost to his eyes and again fell away so that it seemed to drop from under his feet-at last he reached the long French doors, with their drawn curtains. He opened the door suddenly and thereby surprised the secretary, who was a most dignified and rather nervous gentleman, into laying his hand on a heavy inkwell.

"I wish to see the King," said Henri in a loud tone. Because at that moment the secretary, lamp and inkwell and all, retired suddenly to a very great distance, as if one had viewed them through the reverse end of an opera glass.

The secretary knew Henri. He, too, eyed him curiously.

"The King has retired, monsieur."

"I think," said Henri in a dangerous tone, "that he will see me."

To tell the truth, the secretary rather thought so too. There was a strange rumor going round, to the effect that the boy had followed a woman to England at a critical time. Which would have been a pity, the secretary thought. There were so many women, and so few men like Henri.

The secretary considered gravely. Henri was by that time in a chair, but it moved about so that he had to hold very tight to the arms. When he looked up again the secretary had picked up his soft black hat and was at the door.

"I shall inquire," he said. Henri saluted him stiffly, with his left hand, as he went out.

The secretary went to His Majesty's equerry, who was in the next house playing solitaire and trying to forget the family he had left on the other side of the line.

So it was that in due time Henri again traversed miles of path and pavement, between tall borders of wild sea grass, miles which perhaps were a hundred yards. And went round the screen, and-found the King on the hearthrug. But when he drew himself stiffly to attention he overdid the thing rather and went over backward with a crash.

He was up again almost immediately, very flushed and uncomfortable. After that he kept himself in hand, but the King, who had a way all his own of forgetting his divine right to rule, and a great many other things-the King watched him gravely.

Henri sat in a chair and made a clean breast of it. Because he was feeling rather strange he told a great many things that an agent of the secret service is hardly expected to reveal to his king. He mentioned, for instance, the color of Sara Lee's eyes, and the way she bandaged, like one who had been trained.

Once, in the very middle of his narrative, where he had put the letter from the Front in his pocket and decided to go to England anyhow, he stopped and hummed René's version of Tipperary. Only a bar or two. Then he remembered.

But one thing brought him round with a start.

"Then," said the King slowly, "Jean was not with you?"

Only he did not call him Jean. He gave him his other name, which, like Henri's, is not to be told.

Henri's brain cleared then with the news that Jean was missing. When, somewhat later, he staggered out of the villa, it was under royal instructions to report to the great hospital along the sea front and near by, and there to go to bed and have a doctor. Indeed, because the boy's eyes were wild by that time, the equerry went along and held his arm. But that was because Henri was in open revolt, and while walking steadily enough showed a tendency to bolt every now and then.

He would stop on the way and argue, though one does not argue easily with an equerry.

"I must go," he would say fretfully. "God knows where he is. He'd never give me up if I were the one."

And once he shook off the equerry violently and said:

"Let go of me, I tell you! I'll come back and go to bed when I've found him."

The equerry soothed him like a child.

An English nurse took charge of Henri in the hospital, and put him to bed. He was very polite to her, and extremely cynical. She sat in a chair by his bed and held the key of the room in her hand. Once he thought she was Sara Lee, but that was only for a moment. She did not look like Sara Lee. And she was suspicious, too; for when he asked her what she could put in her left hand that she could not put in her right, she moved away and placed the door key on the stand, out of reach.

However, toward morning she dozed. There was steady firing at Nieuport and the windows shook constantly. An ambulance came in, followed by a stirring on the lower floor. Then silence. He got up then and secured the key. There was no time for dressing, because she was a suspicious person and likely to waken at any time. He rolled his clothing into a bundle and carried it under his well arm. The other was almost useless.

The ambulance was still waiting outside, at the foot of the staircase. There were voices and lights in the operating room, forward along the tiled hall. Still in his night clothing, Henri got into the ambulance and threw his uniform behind him. Then he got the car under way.

Outside the village he paused long enough to dress. His head was amazingly clear. He had never felt so sure of himself before. As to his errand he had no doubt whatever. Jean had learned that he had crossed the channel. Therefore Jean had taken up his work-Jean, who had but one eye and was as clumsy as a bear. The thought of Jean crawling through the German trenches set him laughing until he ended with a sob.

It was rather odd about the ambulance. It did not keep the road very well. Sometimes it was on one side and sometimes on the other. It slid as though the road were greased. And after a time Henri made an amazing discovery. He was not alone in the car.

He looked back, without stopping, and the machine went off in a wide arc. He brought it back again, grinning.

"Thought you had me, didn't you?" he observed to the car in general, and the engine in particular. "Now no tricks!"

There was a wounded man in the car. He had had morphia and he was very comfortable. He was not badly hurt, and he considered that he was being taken to Calais. He was too tired to talk, and the swinging of the car rather interested him. He would doze and waken and doze again. But at last he heard something that made him rise on his elbow.

It was the hammering of the big guns.

He called Henri's attention to this, but Henri said:

"Lie down, Jean, and don't talk. We'll make it yet."

The wounded man intended to make a protest, but he went to sleep instead.

They had reached the village now where was the little house of mercy. The ambulance rolled and leaped down the street, with both lights full on, which was forbidden, and came to a stop at the door. The man inside was grunting then, and Henri, whose head had never been so clear, got out and went round to the rear of the car.

"Now, out with you, comrade!" he said. "I have made an error, but it is immaterial. Can you walk?"

He lighted a cigarette, and the man inside saw his burning eyes and shaking hands. Even through the apathy of the morphia he felt a thrill of terror. He could walk. He got out while Henri pounded at the door.

"*Attention!*" he called. "*Attention!*"

Then he hummed an air of the camps:

> Trou là là, ça ne va guère;
> Trou là là, ça ne va pas.

When he heard steps inside Henri went back to the ambulance. He got in and drove it, lights and all, down the street.

> Trou là là, ça ne va guère;
> Trou là là, ça ne va pas.

Somewhere down the road beyond the poplar trees he abandoned the ambulance. They found it there the next morning, or rather what was left of it. Evidently its two unwinking eyes had got on the Germans' nerves.

Early the next morning a Saxon regiment, standing on the firing step ready for what the dawn might bring forth, watched the mist rise from the water in front of them. It shone on a body in a Belgian uniform, lying across their wire, and very close indeed.

Now the Saxons are not Prussians, so no one for sport fired at the body. Which was rather a good thing, because it moved slightly and stirred. And then in a loud voice, which is an unusual thing for bodies to possess, it began to sing:

Trou là là, ça ne va guère;
Trou là là, ça ne va pas.

XXVIII

Late in August Sara Lee broke her engagement with Harvey. She had been away, at Cousin Jennie's, for a month, and for the first time since her return she had had time to think. In the little suburban town there were long hours of quiet when Cousin Jennie mended on the porch and Aunt Harriet, enjoying a sort of reflected glory from Sara Lee, presided at Red Cross meetings.

Sara Lee decided to send for Harvey, and he came for a week-end, arriving pathetically eager, but with a sort of defiance too. He was determined to hold her, but to hold her on his own terms.

Aunt Harriet had been vaguely uneasy, but Harvey's arrival seemed to put everything right. She even kissed him when he came, and took great pains to carry off Cousin Jennie when she showed an inclination toward conversation and a seat on the porch.

Sara Lee had made a desperate resolve. She intended to lay all her cards on the table. He should know all that there was to know. If, after that, he still wanted to hold her-but she did not go so far. She was so sure he would release her.

It was a despairing thing to do, but she was rather despairing those days. There had been no letter from Henri or from Jean. She had written them both several times, to Dunkirk, to the Savoy in London, to the little house near the Front. But no replies had come. Yet mail was going through. Mabel Andrews' letters from Boulogne came regularly.

When August went by, with no letters save Harvey's, begging her to come back, she gave up at last. In the little church on Sundays, with Jennie on one side and Aunt Harriet on the other, she voiced small silent prayers-that the thing she feared had not happened. But she could not think of Henri as not living. He was too strong, too vital.

She did not understand herself those days. She was desperately unhappy. Sometimes she wondered if it would not be easier to know the truth, even if that truth comprehended the worst.

Once she received, from some unknown hand, a French journal, and pored over it for days with her French dictionary, to find if it contained any news. It was not until a week later that she received a letter from Mabel, explaining that she had sent the journal, which contained a description of her hospital.

All of Harvey's Sunday she spent in trying to bring her courage to the point of breaking the silence he had imposed on her, but it was not until evening that she succeeded. The house was empty. The family had gone to church. On the veranda, with the heavy scent of phlox at night permeating the still air, Sara Lee made her confession. She began at the beginning. Harvey did not stir-until she told of the way she had stowed away to cross the channel. Then he moved.

"This fellow who planned that for you-did you ever see him again?"

"He met me in Calais."

"And then what?"

"He took me to Dunkirk in his car. Such a hideous car, Harvey-all wrecked. It had been under fire again and again. I —"

"He took you to Dunkirk! Who was with you?"

"Just Jean, the chauffeur."

"I like his nerve! Wasn't there in all that Godforsaken country a woman to take with you? You and this-What was his name, anyhow?"

"I can't tell you that, Harvey."

"Look here!" he burst out. "How much of this aren't you going to tell? Because I want it all or not at all."

"I can't tell you his name. I'm only trying to make you understand the way I feel about things. His name doesn't matter." She clenched her hands in the darkness. "I don't think he is alive now."

He tried to see her face, but she turned it away.

"Dead, eh? What makes you think that?"

"I haven't heard from him."

"Why should you hear from him?" His voice cut like a knife. "Look at me. Why should he write to you?"

"He cared for me, Harvey."

He sat in a heavy silence which alarmed her.

"Don't be angry, please," she begged. "I couldn't bear it. It wasn't my fault, or his either."

"The damned scoundrel!" said Harvey thickly.

But she reached over and put a trembling hand over his lips.

"Don't say that," she said. "Don't! I won't allow you to. When I think what may have happened to him, I —" Her voice broke.

"Go on," Harvey said in cold tones she had never heard before. "Tell it all, now you've begun it. God knows I didn't want to hear it. He took you to the hotel at Dunkirk, the way those foreigners take their women. And he established you in the house at the Front, I suppose, like a—"

Sara Lee suddenly stood up and drew off her ring.

"You needn't go on," she said quietly. "I had a decision to make to-night, and I have made it. Ever since I came home I have been trying to go back to where we were before I left. It isn't possible. You are what you always were, Harvey. But I've changed. I can't go back."

She put the ring into his hand.

"It isn't that you don't love me. I think you do. But I've been thinking things over. It isn't only to-night, or what you just said. It's because we don't care for the same things, or believe in them."

"But-if we love each other—"

"It's not that, either. I used to feel that way. A home, and some one to care about, and a little pleasure and work."

"That ought to be enough, honey?"

He was terrified. His anger was gone. He placed an appealing hand on her arm, and as she stood there in the faint starlight the wonder of her once again got him by the throat. She had that sort of repressed eagerness, that look of being poised for flight, that had always made him feel cheap and unworthy.

"Isn't that enough, honey?" he repeated.

"Not now," she said, her eyes turned toward the east. "These are great days, Harvey. They are greater and more terrible than any one can know who has not been there. I've been there and I know. I haven't the right to all this peace and comfort when I know how things are going over there."

Down the quiet street of the little town service was over. The last hymn had been sung. Through the open windows came the mellow sound of the minister's voice in benediction, too far away to be more than a tone, like a single deep note of the organ. Sara Lee listened. She knew the words he was saying, and she listened with her eyes turned to the east:

> "The peace of God that passeth all understanding be and abide with you all, forevermore. Amen."

Sara Lee listened, and from the step below her Harvey watched her with furtive, haggard eyes. He had not heard the benediction.

"The peace of God!" she said slowly. "There is only one peace of God, Harvey, and that is service. I am going back."

"Service!" he scoffed. "You are going back to him!"

"I'm afraid he is not there any more. I am going back to work. But if he is there—"

Harvey slid the ring into his pocket. "What if he's not there," he demanded bitterly. "If you think, after all this, that I'm going to wait, on the chance of your coming back to me, you're mistaken. I've been a laughing stock long enough."

In the light of her new decision Sara Lee viewed him for the first time with the pitiless eyes of women who have lost a faith. She saw him for what he was, not deliberately cruel, not even unkindly, but selfish, small, without vision. Harvey was for his own fireside, his office, his little family group. His labor would always be for himself and his own. Whereas Sara Lee was, now and forever, for all the world, her hands consecrated to bind up its little wounds and to soothe its great ones. Harvey craved a cheap and easy peace. She wanted no peace except that bought by service, the peace of a tired body, the peace of the little house in Belgium where, after days of torture, weary men found quiet and ease and the cheer of the open door.

XXIX

Late in October Sara Lee went back to the little house of mercy; went unaccredited, and with her own money. She had sold her bit of property.

In London she went to the Traverses, as before. But with a difference too. For Sara Lee had learned the strangeness of the English, who are slow to friendships but who never forget. Indeed a telegram met her at Liverpool asking her to stop with them in London. She replied, refusing, but thanking them, and saying she would call the next afternoon.

Everything was the same at Morley's: Rather a larger percentage of men in uniform, perhaps; greater crowds in the square; a little less of the optimism which in the spring had predicted victory before autumn. But the same high courage, for all that.

August greeted her like an old friend. Even the waiters bowed to her, and upstairs the elderly chambermaid fussed over her like a mother.

"And you're going back!" she exclaimed. "Fancy that, now! You are brave, miss."

But her keen eyes saw a change in Sara Lee. Her smile was the same, but there were times when she forgot to finish a sentence, and she stood, that first morning, for an hour by the window, looking out as if she saw nothing.

She went, before the visit to the Traverses, to the Church of Saint Martin in the Fields. It was empty, save for a woman in a corner, who did not kneel, but sat staring quietly before her. Sara Lee prayed an inarticulate bit of a prayer, that what the Traverses would have to tell her should not be the thing that she feared, but that, if it were, she be given courage to meet it and to go on with her work.

The Traverses would know; Mrs. Cameron was a friend. They would know about Henri, and about Jean. Soon, within the hour, she would learn everything. So she asked for strength, and then sat there for a time, letting the peace of the old church quiet her, as had the broken walls and shattered altar of that other church, across the channel.

It was rather a surprise to Sara Lee to have Mrs. Travers put her arms about her and kiss her. Mr. Travers, too, patted her hand when he took it. But they had, for all that, the reserve of their class. Much that they felt about Sara Lee they did not express even to each other.

"We are so grateful to you," Mrs. Travers said. "I am only one mother, and of course now —" She looked down at her black dress. "But how many others there are who will want to thank you, when this terrible thing is over and they learn about you!"

Mr. Travers had been eying Sara Lee.

"Didn't use you up, did it?" he asked. "You're not looking quite fit."

Sara Lee was very pale just then. In a moment she would know.

"I'm quite well," she said. "I —do you hear from Mrs. Cameron?"

"Frequently. She has worked hard, but she is not young." It was Mrs. Travers who spoke. "She's afraid of the winter there. I rather think, since you want to go back, that she will be glad to turn your domain over to you for a time."

"Then-the little house is still there?"

"Indeed, yes! A very famous little house, indeed. But it is always known as your house. She has felt like a temporary chatelaine. She always thought you would come back."

Tea had come, as before. The momentary stir gave her a chance to brace herself. Mr. Travers brought her cup to her and smiled gently down at her.

"We have a plan to talk over," he said, "when you have had your tea. I hope you will agree to it."

He went back to the hearthrug.

"When I was there before," Sara Lee said, trying to hold her cup steady, "there was a young Belgian officer who was very kind to me. Indeed, all the credit for what I did belongs to him. And since I went home I haven't heard —"

Her voice broke suddenly. Mr. Travers glanced at his wife. Not for nothing had Mrs. Cameron written her long letters to these old friends, in the quiet summer afternoons when the sun shone down on the lifeless street before the little house.

"I'm afraid we have bad news for you." Mrs. Travers put down her untasted tea. "Or rather, we have no news. Of course," she added, seeing Sara Lee's eyes, "in this war no news may be the best-that is, he may be a prisoner."

"That," Sara Lee heard herself say, "is impossible. If they captured him they would shoot him."

Mrs. Travers nodded silently. They knew Henri's business, too, by that time, and that there was no hope for a captured spy.

"And-Jean?"

They did not know of Jean; so she told them, still in that far-away voice. And at last Mrs. Travers brought an early letter of Mrs. Cameron's and read a part of it aloud.

"He seems to have been delirious," she read, holding her reading glasses to her eyes. "A friend of his, very devoted to him, was missing, and he learned this somehow.

"He escaped from the hospital and got away in an ambulance. He came straight here and wakened us. There had been a wounded man in the machine, and he left him on our doorstep. When I got to the door the car was going wildly toward the Front, with both lamps lighted. We did not understand then, of course, and no one thought of following it. The ambulance was found smashed by a shell the next morning, and at first we thought that he had been in it. But there was no sign that he had been, and that night one of the men from the trenches insisted that he had climbed out of a firing trench where the soldier stood, and had gone forward, bareheaded, toward the German lines.

"I am afraid it was the end. The men, however, who all loved him, do not think so. It seems that he has done miracles again and again. I understand that along the whole Belgian line they watch for him at night. The other night a German on reconnoissance got very close to our wire, and was greeted not by shots but by a wild hurrah. He was almost paralyzed with surprise. They brought him here on the way back to the prison camp, and he still looked dazed."

Sara Lee sat with her hands clenched. Mrs. Travers folded the letter and put it back into its envelope.

"How long ago was that?" Sara Lee asked in a low tone. "Because, if he was coming back at all —"

"Four months."

Suddenly Sara Lee stood up.

"I think I ought to tell you," she said with a dead-white face, "that I am responsible. He cared for me; and I was in love with him too. Only I didn't know it then. I let him bring me to England, because —I suppose it was because I loved him. I didn't think then that it was that. I was engaged to a man at home."

"Sit down," said Mr. Travers. "My dear child, nothing can be your fault."

"He came with me, and the Germans got through. He had had word, but —"

"Have you your salts?" Mr. Travers asked quietly of his wife.

"I'm not fainting. I'm only utterly wretched."

The Traverses looked at each other. They were English. They had taken their own great loss quietly, because it was an individual grief and must not be intruded on the sorrow of a nation. But they found this white-faced girl infinitely appealing, a small and fragile figure, to whose grief must be added, without any fault of hers, a bitter and lasting remorse.

Sara Lee stood up and tried to smile.

"Please don't worry about me," she said. "I need something to do, that's all. You see, I've been worrying for so long. If I can get to work and try to make up I'll not be so hopeless. But I am not quite hopeless, either," she added hastily. It was as though by the very word she had consigned Henri to death. "You see, I am like the men; I won't give him up. And perhaps some night he will come across from the other side, out of the dark."

Mr. Travers took her back to the hotel. When he returned from paying off the taxi he found her looking across at the square.

"Do you remember," she asked him, "the time when the little donkey was hurt over there?"

"I shall never forget it."

"And the young officer who ran out when I did, and shot the poor thing?"

Mr. Travers remembered.

"That was he-the man we have been speaking of."

For the first time that day her eyes filled with tears.

Sara Lee, at twenty, was already living in her memories.

So again the lights went down in front, and the back drop became but a veil, and invisible. And to Sara Lee there came back again some of the characters of the early *mise en scène* —marching men, forage wagons, squadrons of French cavalry escorting various staffs, commandeered farm horses with shaggy fetlocks fastened in rope corrals, artillery rumbling along rutted roads which shook the gunners almost off the limbers.

Nothing was changed-and everything. There was no René to smile his adoring smile, but Marie came out, sobbing and laughing, and threw herself into the girl's arms. The little house was the same, save for a hole in the kitchen wall. There were the great piles of white bowls and the shining kettles. There was the corner of her room, patched by René's hands, now so long quiet. A few more shell holes in the street, many more little crosses in the field near the poplar trees, more Allied aëroplanes in the air-that was all that was changed.

But to Sara Lee everything was changed, for all that. The little house was grave and still, like a house of the dead. Once it had echoed to young laughter, had resounded to the noise and excitement of Henri's every entrance. Even when he was not there it was as though it but waited for him to stir it into life, and small echoes of his gayety had seemed to cling to its old walls.

Sara Lee stood on the doorstep and looked within. She had come back. Here she would work and wait, and if in the goodness of providence he should come back, here he would find her, all the empty months gone and forgotten.

If he did not —

"I shall still be calling you, and waiting," he had written. She, too, would call and wait, and if not here, then surely in the fullness of time which is eternity the call would be answered.

In October Sara Lee took charge again of the little house. Mrs. Cameron went back to England, but not until the Traverses' plan had been revealed. They would support the little house, as a memorial to the son who had died. It was, Mrs. Travers wrote, the finest tribute they could offer to his memory, that night after night tired and ill and wounded men might find sanctuary, even for a little time, under her care.

Luxuries began to come across the channel, food and dressings and tobacco. Knitted things, too; for another winter was coming, and already the frost lay white on the fields in the mornings. The little house took on a new air of prosperity. There were days when it seemed almost swaggering with opulence.

It had need of everything, however. With the prospect of a second winter, when an advance was impossible, the Germans took to hammering again. Bombardment was incessant. The little village was again under suspicion, and there came days of terror when it seemed as though even the fallen masonry must be reduced to powder. The church went entirely.

By December Sara Lee had ceased to take refuge during the bombardments. The fatalism of the Front had got her. She would die or live according to the great plan, and nothing could change that. She did not greatly care which, except for her work, and even that she felt could be carried on by another as well.

There was no news of Henri, but once the King's equerry, going by, had stopped to see her and had told her the story.

"He was ill, undoubtedly," he said. "Even when he went to London he was ill, and not responsible. The King understands that. He was a brave boy, mademoiselle."

But the last element of hope seemed to go with that verification of his illness. He was delirious, and he had gone in that condition into the filthy chill waters of the inundation. Well and sane there had been a chance, but plunging wild-eyed and reckless, into that hell across, there was none.

She did her best in the evenings to be cheerful, to take the place, in her small and serious fashion, of Henri's old gayety. But the soldiers whispered among themselves that mademoiselle was in grief, as they were, for the blithe young soldier who was gone.

What hope Sara Lee had had died almost entirely early in December. On the evening of a day when a steady rain had turned the roads into slimy pitfalls, and the ditches to canals, there came, brought by a Belgian corporal, the man who swore that Henri had passed him in his trench while the others slept, had shoved him aside, which was unlike his usual courtesy, and had climbed out over the top.

To Sara Lee this Hutin told his story. A short man with a red beard and a kindly smile that revealed teeth almost destroyed from neglect, he was at first diffident in the extreme.

"It was the captain, mademoiselle," he asserted. "I know him well. He has often gone on his errands from near my post. I am" —he smiled —"I am usually in the front line."

"What did he do?"

"He had no cap, mademoiselle. I thought that was odd. And as you know-he does not wear his own uniform on such occasions. But he wore his own uniform, so that at first I did not know what he intended."

"Later on," she asked, "you-did you hear anything?"

"The usual sniping, mademoiselle. Nothing more."

"He went through the inundation?"

"How else could he go? Through the wire first, at the barrier, where there is an opening, if one knows the way, I saw him beyond it, by the light of a fusee. There is a road there, or what was once a road. He stood there. Then the lights went out."

XXX

On a wild night in January Sara Lee inaugurated a new branch of service. There had been a delay in sending up to the Front the men who had been on rest, and an incessant bombardment held the troops prisoners in their trenches.

A field kitchen had been destroyed. The men were hungry, disheartened, wet through. They needed her, she felt. Even the little she could do would help. All day she had made soup, and at evening Marie led from its dilapidated stable the little horse that Henri had once brought up, trundling its cart behind it. The boiler of the cart was scoured, a fire lighted in the fire box. Marie, a country girl, harnessed the shaggy little animal, but with tears of terror.

"You will be killed, mademoiselle," she protested, weeping.

"But I have gone before. Don't you remember the man whose wife was English, and how I wrote a letter for him before he died?"

"What will become of the house if you are killed?"

"Dear Marie," said Sara Lee, "that is all arranged for. You will send to Poperinghe for your aunt, and she will come until Mrs. Cameron or some one else can come from England. And you will stay on. Will you promise that?"

Marie promised in a loud wail.

"Of course I shall come back," Sara Lee said, stirring her soup preparatory to pouring it out. "I shall be very careful."

"You will not come back, mademoiselle. You do not care to live, and to such —"

"Those are the ones who live on," said Sara Lee gravely, and poured out her soup.

She went quite alone. There was a great deal of noise, but no shells fell near her. She led the little horse by its head, and its presence gave her comfort. It had a sense that she had not, too, for it kept her on the road.

In those still early days the Belgian trenches were quite accessible from the rear. There were no long tunneled ways to traverse to reach them. One went along through the darkness until the sound of men's voices, the glare of charcoal in a bucket bored with holes, the flicker of a match, told of the buried army almost underfoot or huddled in its flimsy shelters behind the railway embankment.

Beyond the lines a sentry stopped her, hailing her sharply.

"*Qui vive?*"

"It is I," she called through the rain. "I have brought some chocolate and some soup."

He lowered his bayonet.

"Pass, mademoiselle."

She went on, the rumbling of her little cart deadened by the Belgian guns.

Through the near-by trenches that night went the word that near the Repose of the Angels-which was but a hole in the ground and scarcely reposeful-there was to be had hot soup and chocolate and cigarettes. A dozen or so at a time, the men were allowed to come. Officers brought their great capes to keep the girl dry. Boards appeared as if by magic for her to stand on. The rain and the bombardment had both ceased, and a full moon made the lagoon across the embankment into a silver lake.

When the last soup had been dipped from the tall boiler, when the final drops of chocolate had oozed from the faucet, Sara Lee turned and went back to the little house again. But before she went she stood a moment staring across toward that land of the shadow on the other side, where Henri had gone and had not returned.

Once, when the King had decorated her, she had wished that, wherever Uncle James might be, on the other side, he could see what was happening. And now she wondered if Henri could know that she had come back, and was again looking after his men while she waited for that reunion he had so firmly believed in.

Then she led the little horse back along the road.

At the poplar trees she turned and looked behind, toward the trenches. The grove was but a skeleton now, a strange and jagged thing of twisted branches, as though it had died in agony. She stood there while the pony nuzzled her gently. If she called, would he come? But, then, all of life was one call now, for her. She went on slowly.

After that it was not unusual for her to go to the trenches, on such nights as no men could come to the little house. Always she was joyously welcomed, and always on her way back she turned to send from the poplar trees that inarticulate aching call that she had come somehow to believe in.

January, wet and raw, went by; February, colder, with snow, was half over. The men had ceased to watch for Henri over the parapet, and his brave deeds had become fireside tales, to be told at home, if ever there were to be homes again for them.

Then one night Henri came back-came as he had gone, out of the shadows that had swallowed him up; came without so much as the sound of a sniper's rifle to herald him. A strange, thin Henri, close to starvation, dripping water over everything from a German uniform, and very close indeed to death before he called out.

There was wild excitement indeed. Bearded private soldiers, forgetting that name and rank of his which must not be told, patted his thin shoulders. Officers who had lived through such horrors as also may not be told, crowded about him and shook hands with him, and with each other.

It was as though from the graveyard back in the fields had come, alive and smiling, some dearly beloved friend.

He would have told the story, but he was wet and weary.

"That can wait," they said, and led him, a motley band of officers and men intermixed, for once forgetting all decorum, toward the village. They overtook the lines of men who had left the trenches and were moving with their slow and weary gait up the road. The news spread through the column. There were muffled cheers. Figures stepped out of the darkness with hands out. Henri clasped as many as he could.

When with his escort he had passed the men they fell, almost without orders, into columns of four, and swung in behind him. There was no band, but from a thousand throats, yet cautiously until they passed the poplar trees, there gradually swelled and grew a marching song.

Behind Henri a strange guard of honor-muddy, tired, torn, even wounded-they marched and sang:

> Trou là là, ça ne va guère;
> Trou là là, çe ne va pas.

Sara Lee, listening for that first shuffle of many feet that sounded so like the wind in the trees or water over the pebbles of a brook, paused in her work and lifted her head. The rhythm of marching feet came through the wooden shutters. The very building seemed to vibrate with it. And there was a growling sound with it that soon she knew to be the deep voices of singing men.

She went to the door and stood there, looking down the street. Behind her was the warm glow of the lamp, all the snug invitation of the little house.

A group of soldiers had paused in front of the doorway, and from them one emerged-tall, white, infinitely weary-and looked up at her with unbelieving eyes.

After all, there are no words for such meetings. Henri took her hand, still with that sense of unreality, and bent over it. And Sara Lee touched his head as he stooped, because she had called for so long, and only now he had come.

"So you have come back!" she said in what she hoped was a composed tone-because a great many people were listening. He raised his head and looked at her.

"It is you who have come back, mademoiselle."

There was gayety in the little house that night. Every candle was lighted. They were stuck in rows on mantel-shelves. They blazed-and melted into strange arcs-above the kitchen stove. There were cigarettes for everybody, and food; and a dry uniform, rather small, for Henri. Marie wept over her soup, and ran every few moments to the door to see if he was still there. She had kissed him on both cheeks when he came in, and showed signs, every now and then, of doing it again.

Sara Lee did her bandaging as usual, but with shining eyes. And soon after Henri's arrival a dispatch rider set off post haste with certain papers and maps, hurriedly written and drawn. Henri had not only returned, he had brought back information of great value to all the Allied armies.

So Sara Lee bandaged, and in the little room across the way, where no longer Harvey's photograph sat on the mantel, Henri told his story to the officers-of his imprisonment in the German prison at Crefeld; of his finding Jean there, weeks later when he was convalescing from typhoid; of their escape and long wandering; of Jean's getting into Holland, whence he would return by way of England. Of his own business, of what he had done behind the lines after Jean had gone, he said nothing. But his listeners knew and understood.

But his dispatches off, his story briefly told, Henri wandered out among the men again. He was very happy. He had never thought to be so happy. He felt the touch on his sleeves of hard brown, not overclean hands, infinitely tender and caressing; and over there, as though she had never gone, was Sara Lee, slightly flushed and very radiant.

And as though he also had never gone away, Henri pushed into the *salle à manger* and stood before her smiling.

"You bandage well, mademoiselle," he said gayly. "But I? I bandage better! See now, a turn here, and it is done! Does it hurt, Paul?"

The man in the dressing chair squirmed and grinned sheepishly.

"The iodine," he explained. "It is painful."

"Then I shall ask you a question, and you will forget the iodine. Why is a dead German like the tail of a pig?"

Paul failed. The room failed. Even Colonel Lilias confessed himself at fault.

"Because it is the end of the swine," explained Henri, and looked about him triumphantly. A gust of laughter spread through the room and even to the kitchen. A door banged. Henri upset a chair. There was noise again, and gayety in the little house of mercy. And much happiness.

And there I think we may leave them all-Henri and Sara Lee; and Jean of the one eye and the faithful heart; and Marie, with her kettles; and even René, who still in some strange way belonged to the little house, as though it were something too precious to abandon.

The amazing interlude had become the play itself. Never again for Sara Lee would the lights go up in front, and Henri with his adoring eyes and open arms fade into the shadows.

The drama of the war plays on. The Great Playwright sees fit, now and then, to take away some well-beloved players. New faces appear and disappear. The music is the thunder of many guns. Henri still plays his big part, Sara Lee her little one. Yet who shall say, in the end, which one has done the better? There are new and ever new standards, but love remains the chief. And love is Sara Lee's one quality-love of her kind, of tired men and weary, the love that shall one day knit this broken world together. And love of one man.

On weary nights, when Henri is again lost in the shadows, Sara Lee, her work done, the men gone, sits in her little house of mercy and waits. The stars on clear evenings shine down on the roofless buildings, on the rubbish that was once the mill, on the ruined poplar trees, and on the small acre of peace where tiny crosses mark the long sleep of weary soldiers.

And sometimes, though she knows it now by heart, she reads aloud that letter of Henri's to her. It comforts her. It is a promise.

"If that is to be, then think of me, somewhere, perhaps with René by my side, since he, too, loved you. And I shall still be calling you, and waiting. Perhaps, even beyond the stars, they have need of a little house of mercy. And God knows, wherever I am, I shall have need of you."

THE END

www.ingramcontent.com/pod-product-compliance
Lightning Source LLC
Chambersburg PA
CBHW071329130626
46556CB00004B/1818